MY SWAPNA

Tapan Ghosh

First Published in 2022

Becomeshakespeare.com

One Point Six Technologies Pvt Ltd.
119-123, 1st Floor, Building J2, B - Wing, Wadala Truck Terminal,
Wadala East, Mumbai, Maharashtra, India, 400022.
T: +91 8080226699

Wordit Art Fund helps deserving authors publish their work by providing monetary support. To apply for funding, please visit us at www.BecomeShakespeare.com

Visit my website: www.tapanghosh.com

Cover designed by Tushar More

ISBN - 978-93-5559-136-4

To Shom, Raima, and everyone else who has been a part of my life.

Table of Contents

Prologue

This book is a sequel to 'The Saga of Shom and Raima'. In this emotionally packed drama, Harry is the anchor who lives across two generations, one with the legendary love of Shom and Raima, and before that with the love of Cindy and Dilip. His recollections from the age of ten acts as an inspiration for the author to pen this book 'My Swapna'. Swapna is his kindred spirit.

For the first-time readers of the author's works, there is an imminent need to recapitulate the prequel.

1
The Backstory

Harry breaks away from Swapna, as he was in no position to continue their relationship. Swapna was destined to get married to someone rich and more of her age. The man she married became an alcoholic, who made her life miserable and finally died from liver cirrhosis. Although the young widow had many suitors, she held them aside, being deeply in love with Harry. Besides, she had a loving daughter Natasha and the family business to look after.

She dared to import a vibrating dildo because her physical needs were unfulfilled. One day, Natasha returned early from the university, and heard her mother locked up in her room moaning with joy. When she looked through the keyhole, she was aghast at watching her mother fantasize with a dildo. Natasha was disturbed and so she confided with her dearest friend Raima, who consoled her and later they decided to experiment with the dildo, which they did. They panicked when Swapna knocked on their door and they promptly buttoned up and left the dildo on the outside edge of the window. The dildo fell down, and at dawn, an old woman picked it up, was outraged, and threw it in the nearest dustbin. The dildo landed into the empty bin with an impact, making the vibrator come on with strong resonance, causing fear of the bomb that was provoked in everybody's mind because of the recent terrorist attack at the Taj Hotel. It was then that Khush arrived with the fire-fighters and the police van. He flipped over the bin and to everyone's amazement, the dildo threw up a lot of dust. Khush was smart enough to know that it was a dildo. He went ahead to everyone's astonishment and quickly picked it up to switch off the vibrator. As he held it up the crowd went crazy, as if he had diffused a bomb! The camera lights flashed as the reporters were everywhere and Khush became the hero.

Upon a thorough investigation, Khush spotted the apartment and found the person he was seeking to rescue from embarrassment and satisfy her physical needs. She was Swapna; her very first gaze of beauty in need confirmed her sentiments. However, Khush's enthusiasm was in for a disappointment, when she turned her back on him. On the other hand, Raima claimed to own the dildo and she seduced him to think her way. This resulted in an intimate and close relationship between the two, she was only eighteen, and he was forty-five years old.

This affair lasted until Saif Ali, a young man appeared, which ended as soon as she discovered that he was a Pakistani by the name of Iqbal Muhammad, with links to the terrorist Headley – formerly known as Daood Sayed Gilani – whose connections to 26/11 were being traced. He was one of the key suspects for 26/11. She immediately contacted Khush, who was well connected and together they got Saif convicted.

Khush had a childhood friend named Shom. Both were very popular on the streets of Colaba and lived side by side opposite the Strand cinema, one of the most popular theatres in their early childhood days.

Shom and Raima were in touch online, they were faceless on Facebook, where they poured their hearts out. The day they met, they fell in love. Shom was touched by her story, Raima having been a victim of a difficult childhood. After losing her father at the age of three, she assumed charge of her ailing mother. She was brought up by her maternal aunt, and as a young girl, her lustful uncle had sexually assaulted her.

Shom did not like Khush's reactions when he told him about his love. Khush realised that his friend was in a trap. In an attempt to pull him out of there, he planned an unusual adventure, whereby he met an incredibly seductive woman named Aneesha, at a nightclub in Bandra. Khush was shocked when Aneesha revealed that she was Aneesha during night and Anish during the day, so to speak, a she-male. Khush couldn't handle it, and he went off in a hurry.

Raima became the cause of disagreement between the two dear friends and all three confided in Harry, who was seen as their guru, a love guru. Raima was a pure soul and Swapna, her mentor and godmother.

When her ailing mother expired, she rushed to Calcutta to live with her grandparents, who were busy looking for a proper match for her, a *Bangla Babu*. Raima couldn't cope with the pressure and came to Bombay under the pretext of work. Harry gave her a place to live because she was not able to go back to the home where she lived with her suffering mother. In return,

Harry's stars began to shine when he discovered his beloved Swapna through Raima. Raima was like an angel who reunited her godfather and godmother. While Harry and Swapna were in their seventh heaven, Raima and Natasha were ignored.

Moreover, Raima's life was treacherous, because her lecherous uncle watched her closely and had spread the news of the duo Shom and Raima. The duo pledged to respect social norms to avoid harming each other's families. On the other hand, Natasha was quite frustrated that Harry's son Arjun was playing hard to get exactly as Khush did years ago. To escape the chaos, she came to Raima and decided to stay with her in Harry's house. That was the first time Natasha and Raima huddled together after the dildo incident years ago. Raima too was highly receptive because she was in a similar state of mind being without Shom. Natasha pulled a two-headed dildo from her suitcase. It stunned Raima and they were back in the old days, this time without fear or guilt. They kept moving between Raima's bedroom in Colaba and Natasha's, at Altamount Road. At this time, they laid a trap for Raima's uncle. They had him caught and put behind the bars for the attempted rape of Raima in her early teens. Raima managed to get Khush and Harry to help her win the trial, where the scoundrel was locked up for life. It was a big victory when Raima's grandfather realised that his son-in-law was a monster. Amidst all this, Raima managed a huge breakthrough in a leading women's empowerment program in Jaipur, and she relocated.

Anita Gupta, nicknamed Anu, a masseuse, worked in a spa near the Taj hotel, and was Harry's new favourite, courtesy Khush. Anu was indeed a specialist in yoga asanas and stretching that made Harry stronger and left him craving for more after their happy endings. She was destined to occupy Raima's room that was empty, as Raima had moved to Jaipur.

Khush had a very interesting brother-in-law named Shamiq, a gay who was a brilliant sound engineer and the most popular disc jockey. But he was disliked by Anu due to their acquaintance when they both were in their early teens.

While everything was hunky-dory with Harry and the rest, there was an SOS message on Shom's WhatsApp from Raima, who was in Jaipur. Shom called Khush and they both flew off to Jaipur, but as fate would have it, they could not save Raima. She died at the hands of Saif Ali, who had escaped from prison. Shom was devastated; he would have ended his life if it had not been for Raima's dying breath, which wanted Saif dead. Shom vowed to track down Saif and avenge Raima's death and as he was also a national threat. This needed all the planning and active support from Anish/Aneesha and Shamiq. Khush and Harry were in the background. To cut the long matter short the plan was exceptional and executed extraordinarily. Shom was pronounced dead, but the body was Saïf's.

While only Harry, Khush, and Swapna celebrated within themselves, the rest were shocked. In the meantime, Harry entertained the group with a very similar case of Cindy and Dilip where the features of Dilip where those of Raima and Shom are like Cindy's.

The core nature of the three, Shom, Khush, and Harry is the same as the three are positive and women-centric.

However, Shom is emotional and more heart-governed, Khush is a realist and mind-governed. While Harry rules both his heart and mind, and thus maintains a proper balance between the two.

Swapna was the only one to fathom Raima in its entirety because they were similar in all aspects. Swapna was just a lot more mature.

2

Intense grief and ultimate bliss

For Harry, it was a proud moment, a time for celebration—the first in seventy-two years. Nothing, including his engineering achievements came close to what he had experienced in the last few days.

Shom and Raima, the cause of the biggest grief in his life, were also the reason for the special feeling he now experienced. Shaken up early, life had been aimless until he had met an angel who made it so meaningful that he loved her as her own. Everyone around him was mourning her sudden departure, except him. He wondered why. With Shom also gone, his life should have been meaningless; instead, it was more purposeful now. Now, he understood what life was all about. Dilip, his friend from his growing up years, and Raima, were the same person. They did not die. So why should anyone grieve for them? We don't die. We are just born again...

He was thrilled to know that he could explore the mysteries of life. He was adventurous enough to flirt with life and live on the edge, if needed. All his confidence - rather faith in himself - came from his ladylove, because every warrior is empowered by his ladylove, who is always within him, hand in glove.

Swapna was the love of his life, whom he had broken up with as a young man. The world had not been with them. They had decided to give in to the so-called social decrees. To live without each other took the wind out of their sails. They had never expected to meet again, but providence had favoured them. And Harry had met her through Raima. He remembered the day Shom had brought Raima to Radio Club, on the harbour front close to the Taj. No sooner they met, they had bonded like old buddies.

It was quite a sight to watch them in action. Seeing the compassion in Harry's eyes, Raima had felt completely at ease with him. She thought his comments were pure and benevolent.

They often met thereafter, initially with Shom, and later, just the two of them. Harry always found time for Raima, despite his busy schedule. Their interaction was full of positivity, which benefitted them both.

Raima talked about Swapna, who was more than a mother to her. Harry's face lit up at the very mention of Swapna's name. He wanted to hug Raima for this revelation. He wanted to know everything about Swapna. Harry was jubilant when he learned that Swapna was a successful businesswoman. When Raima told him she was a widow of a good-for-nothing alcoholic Harry got the shudders. It reminded him of all the difficulties he had been through for fame and success.

When they eventually met, it was more than a dream come true for both of them. It was nothing short of a miracle. Now it was Raima's turn to be astonished. The intensity of their love was beyond compare. All bygones were forgotten. Time flew as they spent time catching up on the past. When it was time to go, they decided to meet again the next day, at Polly, the most exclusive restaurant at the CCI.

This was a meeting of the souls. They were in a private club, but nevertheless a public place. There was a sense of relief, yet, they had to be aware of their personal responsibilities. Harry had his family, and so did Swapna. The past flashed through their minds. Years ago, they had gradually detached themselves of attachment for each other. Harry had deliberately betrayed Swapna and got married, leaving Swapna with no option but to move on.

They had managed to keep themselves apart in terms of worldly affection. That was the reason they were not aware of each other's whereabouts, till Raima brought them together. All they had was pure love for each other. Only Lord Krishna could have told them the means to detached attachment.

"What a coincidence!" said Swapna, breaking his train of thought. "We continue to have Raima between us."

"Coincidence is beyond logical explanation, hence understood only by the illogical part of the mind called heart," replied Harry.

"Coincidence is one of His ways to send us a message. We have to understand the underlying divine idea."

"True. The message seems very clear. Our separation is over. Because our love has withstood the negativity of material attachment."

They were so engrossed in each other that the waiter had to draw their attention to the menu.

They recovered quickly and least interested in food, they ordered without wasting time. For the first time, Harry looked at Swapna closely. She was still young, beautiful, and just as desirable. This had skipped his attention at the previous meeting. He wondered why that would happen. Outwardly, looks were all about attachment, and so that had taken a backseat to the flow of energy between the two souls.

The loud knock on the door snapped Harry back to the present. Swapna and Arjun entered the master bedroom.

"Dad, Khush has been wanting to meet you for a long time," announced Arjun.

"Anita and I have told everyone the entire story of how you knew Cindy and Dilip, who were Shom and Raima in their previous birth. And how you have lost Raima/Dilip twice in your lifetime," said Swapna.

"Khush is so worried about you that he has already downed two pegs of single malts. He wants to meet you," added Arjun.

"Call Khush immediately while I change into something respectable," announced Harry.

3

Raima, the angel

Harry was in Calcutta to explore some new business prospects.

His house in Calcutta was teeming with guests. Some were in the hall, while others were in the beautiful porch outside it. Khush and Aneesha had come from Bombay. Sanjib and Anuradha had driven down from Ballygunge. Anita had arrived a fortnight earlier, but Natasha and Arjun had been around for a while.

It was a time for reckoning after the grief that had overcome them all. Harry and Swapna had been the closest to Raima. Harry felt a special bond because Raima had stayed with him for a while. And, in her previous birth as Dilip, she had been his mentor. The guests wanted Harry to unravel the connection between Shom, Raima, and the people they were in their previous lives.

Seeing Arjun all alone, Swapna joined him in mixing around with the guests, as Natasha was too preoccupied with being the centre of attraction. Khush was overjoyed on seeing Harry and hugged him. Harry enquired about his newfound love, Aneesha.

"So, you guys have been going through a lot of adventure. You started with Aneesha, while Shom ended with Raima."

"I know that Arjun has kept you quite updated!"

"Yes. And Shom told me about her heroic deeds. Okay, now give me a joint, I need to change my mood and make myself presentable."

Khush pulled out his vaporiser and both started vaping, inhaling the clean vapour, a good mix of CBD and THC.

Once done, they came down the stairs to join the guests. Harry noticed Natasha and Anita in the porch, dressed in white, as per the Hindu custom for widows. They waved to him and he waved back. Sanjib and Anuradha were with them. Harry had a pleasant surprise when a gorgeous looking woman came up and hugged him. It was Aneesha. Harry liked her instantly. She was almost as tall as he was and was graced with a perfect body.

 The guests in the porch trooped into the hall. Harry met them individually, receiving their condolences for Shom and Raima. Swapna requested a minute's silence to pray for the departed souls. Later, each one of them opened their hearts and spoke a few words.

Anuradha held on to Sanjib, breaking down as she spoke.

"I hope my late brother Sudip forgives me, if I have faulted in looking after Raima. She was just a child when her mother became bedridden. Being married to an inconsiderate man, there were times when I felt I wasn't doing enough for my niece. Raima was an angel who released me from my marital shackles."

"She was undoubtedly an angel. She made my dreams come true and I couldn't even thank her," said Sanjib.

Harry patted him on the back.

"Sanjib, I have heard a lot about you. Anuradha and you make a lovely pair. I am sure Raima felt the same."

Natasha spoke next. "I judged her rather unkindly, but I loved her."

"Shom said that I reminded him of a younger, aggressive Raima; Natasha says the same thing," added Anita.

"You are still Raima for me," chipped in Natasha.

It was Khush's turn to speak.

"Shom and I were best friends from the Strand cinema locality of Colaba. Raima sought my help in the Saif Ali case. Aneesha and I did all that we could to track Saif Ali for Shom."

Aneesha nodded.

"I admired Shom for being such a gentleman. He told me how much Khush loved me. Now, thanks to him, Khush and I are back together."

Aneesha's expression and purity impressed Harry.

"You made the capture of Saif Ali possible, Aneesha."

"And you are the perfect blend of Khush and Shom," said Aneesha, returning the compliment.

Before Harry could reply, Swapna stepped forward to say her bit.

"Harry and I have been in love for nearly four decades now. I was only 14 and Harry 28, when we first met. Ours was a clandestine affair and we knew that we would have to part. But all our efforts failed. Harry curtailed my plan to elope, repeatedly. He made me realise that it would be impossible to live in this world with guilt. My

father and I were too attached to each other and Harry felt he was far too orthodox a man to accept a penniless son-in-law, who was much older than I was.

Harry felt my father was likely to commit suicide or suffer a heart attack, if I did not call off the relationship. Harry thwarted all our attempts to end our lives. We ended up making a huge sacrifice, exactly like Anuradha and Sanjib. Only my angel Raima brought us all together. And now she is no more."

Arjun stepped in to console Swapna.

"Raima was heaven sent to so many. She was a great soul and led a purposeful life. I only knew her as a fighter and my well-wisher. One who fought every wrong. She sacrificed her life to be with Shom. Both are in bliss now. Everything good happens after big sacrifices are made; Anuradha-Sanjib, Shom-Raima, Cindy-Dilip, Swapna-Harry, and now Aneesha-Khush."

"Well said, son!" said Harry, placing his hand on Arjun's shoulder. *"There is a higher purpose to life that goes beyond our lifetime and is eternal. Nature's logic is different from the worldly one. Raima's dad, and before that, Dilip's mom died when their children were very young. I mentored Raima the way Dilip Dada mentored me. This is how karma balances out. In the same way, I balanced out with Shom who worked for me, for what Cindy did for me. She was my teacher, trainer, and well-wisher. The past few days have immensely benefited us in acquiring the wisdom of the beyond."*

Harry's eyes were moist and his voice choked with emotion. He looked way. He was not his jovial self. Tears trickled down his cheeks as he tried to smile away his embarrassment. He was in bliss.

"There is a purpose to everything that happens. Nothing is incidental! The karma may be illogical, yet, it is viable, because it is His purpose. We must practise detached attachment."

"What's that?" enquired Aneesha.

"Exactly what we are doing now. Loving more and caring less," replied Harry.

"Basically, being bindaas in love," said Khush.

"Exactly!" said Harry spiritedly.

That was the first laughter in the emotion-charged environment. Everyone felt relaxed and Arjun busied himself making everyone a drink. Swapna cozied up with Khush, who had been dying to be with her since the dildo incident. Harry and Aneesha were together in another corner.

4
New pairings

Khush looked quite amused when Swapna of all the people, sat down beside him with an inviting smile. Everyone had already left. Anuradha and Sanjib had to leave early to be with Anuradha's grief-stricken parents. Raima had been their only grandchild. Their survival now depended on Anuradha and Sanjib's marriage. Natasha, Anita, and Arjun went to the Calcutta Club. Khush found the right moment to corner Swapna and question her about something he had wanted to know for a long time.

"You have never encouraged me to talk to you, you have always avoided me," he remarked.

"I have always avoided you because that is how I react to people like you," replied Swapna.

"What's wrong with people like me and why the sudden change of heart?"

"To answer your first question, you behaved like a dog that runs after a bitch on heat. You hurt my feelings the very first day I set my eyes on you from my window. That day when I lost my dildo, you got the media to exhibit it to the world and then you had the gall to approach me. You wanted to satisfy the owner of the dido. You expected me to come out in the open and be laid. I thank my

stars that my angel Raima came to my rescue. She seduced you into believing the dildo belonged to her.”

Khush did not know where to look; he regretted having started the conversation. Swapna was glad to see his sorry face.

“Now to answer your second question, I have to say that you have changed a lot over the years. This could be because of Harry’s influence. I can vouch for it because I am probably the biggest gainer of Harry’s goodwill. Although I have never admitted this to him or to myself, the truth just came out today.”

“Why today?”

“Perhaps because we all opened our hearts to Raima’s soul.”

“You are right about Harry’s influence on me. He has lived life to the fullest and there is a lot to learn from him. But for him, I couldn’t have considered running Shom’s business. You are also right about today being a special day. But how did you benefit from him?”

“I wouldn’t have been able to go through my disastrous marriage, bring up my kid, and look after my business single-handed, had it not been for his firmness and wisdom.”

“But Harry was not around at that time. You did everything on your own.”

“He saw to it that he was not around, otherwise; I would have remained dependent. It took me almost forty years. The first ten with him and the rest without him. I only started paying heed to what he used to say when he was not there to say it anymore. I gathered courage and disciplined myself. It has taken me several years to be

independent of him and to kill my attachment for him. Today, we are in love without being possessive about each other. This is detached love. These forty years of detachment have made our love strong and unconditional."

"Detached love, unconditional love; I know a lot about this, but what has it done for you?"

"I have met Harry only recently after years of being apart. Our relationship – if you can call it that – is drastically different now. We are independent of each other and lead our own lives. I go out with my male friends as I did while we were apart, and he does the same with his female friends. We accept each other's separate enjoyments when we talk about them. We care a lot about each other in a carefree way. Ours is a bindaas love. I heard about being bindaas from Harry when I was fourteen, but it's only now that I know what it really means."

"Oh yes! Bindaas is Harry's favourite word and what you tell me is amazing. I have a lot to learn, but I don't think and I don't analyse. I am just bindaas!"

"Yes. Aneesha is a good soul to learn from."

Swapna moved a bit closer to Khush and right at that moment, the music began to play. They looked up to find Harry with Aneesha on the dance floor, signalling them to join the party. Swapna saw Khush looking at her eagerly and she pulled him on to the dance floor.

Aneesha was doing the salsa on the Mombomania track and Harry was taking the lead, challenging Aneesha with every move.

She displayed unbelievable dancing skills and was more than a match for him. Khush was not into dancing; he just managed to hold on to Swapna while they watched the show.

When the track ended, they applauded and Swapna changed to a slow dancing track that called for a physical closeness. The scene on the floor changed. Now, there were two couples dancing in close contact.

5

Calling a Blackmailer's Bluff

The dancing went on for a while before they wound up with an exhausting track called, '*The Time of My Life*'. Swapna and Aneesha were still competing with one another, but Khush and Harry were completely exhausted. They were amused to see the women leave the room immediately after the track ended.

Harry patted Khush on his shoulders as if to say, "Let them have it out, while we relax." Khush caught on. They settled down with a drink, while the women were busy freshening up in the washroom.

"Where did you disappear?" asked Harry as the women returned.

"We spent some time together," replied Swapna.

"I am eager to know, how," said Khush.

"What were you thinking Khush?" enquired Aneesha.

"I don't think that much, I am bindaas," replied Khush.

"Why did your eyes sparkle? Maybe you were thinking about what they did together. Tell us, be bindaas," urged Harry.

"I was thinking about the two of you in a physical encounter," replied Khush, his gaze firmly on Swapna.

"Women don't have a one-track mind. Men think of such things because they are taboo. Women have graver concerns, as the preying eyes of men never leave them alone," replied Swapna.

"That's interesting, Swapna, because I can think both like a man and a woman. I understand both viewpoints and desires. In the ultimate analysis they are both good, but insecurity, greed and power has come in our way. This is what we have done to ourselves; the purity within us has been destroyed," said Aneesha.

"This has happened due to the taboo imposed by godly people; the agents of God, who want to exercise control," responded Swapna.

"The purity of physical intimacy has been overpowered by words such as adultery and infidelity. Why should we suppress the greatest joy granted to us and not indulge ourselves to outgrow it?" asked Harry.

"Adultery is no longer a criminal offence in India," added Khush.

"I just remembered how you put the hotel manager who was extorting money from innocent lovers, behind bars," said Harry.

"It was my friend Zareena, who was in love with Farook, another friend," recalled Khush.

"You mean, Freddie Mercury?" enquired Aneesha.

"No silly, this Farook is alive and of Harry's age. Anyway, this manager, Subodh Pal, quit his job after a rift with the owner's son, who had recently joined the business, armed with an MBA degree from Harvard. To spite the management, he took along information on all couples who stayed at the hotel on an hourly basis. Soon, he

began to blackmail them. Zareena and Farook happened to be one of them. I roped in my buddy, the Chief of Police and we laid a trap for the blackmailer who was due to visit Zareena's house to collect the hush money. Coincidentally, this happened on September 27 last year, a couple of hours after the Supreme Court ruled that adultery was no longer an offence," said Khush.

"I remember this," recalled Swapna. *"Raima was thrilled because it gave women equal rights. The Supreme Court called the law unconstitutional because it treated the husband as the master. But why did Zareena, not Farook approach you for help?"*

"Farook felt awkward; Zareena is his neighbour's wife," replied Khush.

"While the manager was counting the money, Zareena asked him about the other people he had blackmailed. He rattled off the details and we have the evidence on video, thanks to a secret camera we had planted in the room. He was immediately arrested. The joke was on him because, in trying to build a case of adultery, he revealed his ignorance of the Supreme Court ruling. The news was in the papers only the next day. He is now serving a prison sentence."

Harry laughed and patted Khush on the back. Just then. Arjun walked in with Natasha and Anita clinging to him.

6

Like father, like son

"Your son is a handsome bloke," remarked Aneesha, admiring Arjun.

He looked a bit confused, as he didn't know her well enough. She had the look of an athlete. Arjun watched her long and shapely legs as she moved about in the hall.

What Arjun admired most was the shapely posterior and non-bulging bosom, yet firm and jutting out. Khush was the lucky one, he thought.

As Arjun's eye followed Aneesha, Anita noticed it and said, *"Like father, like son."* Everyone nodded in agreement, while Anita and Harry smiled at each other.

"How's your spa doing?" asked Harry.

"It has closed down," said Anita grimly. *"The owner decided to shut the business due to reducing patronage. We had some regular clients like Shom and there were others like you and Arjun, who visited sparingly."*

"What are you up to, Anita? Why are you dragging my dad's name into this?" demanded Arjun.

"It had an impeccable reputation. We had the Who's Who of SoBo as our customers."

"I don't know, I heard a few things."

"I loved Shom. But you can't blame the spa for what you heard from Khush."

"What's the fuss about?" interjected Harry. *"Arjun, don't be harsh on Anita. Let's not be judgemental."*

"I agree," chipped in Swapna. *"That's the way to live life."*

"Arjun is just being protective about his dad," said Khush.

"Now tell me, Anita, have your dues been settled?" enquired Harry.

"I have got most of it; thirty per cent of the profits amount to forty lakhs, of which Mariwala has given me thirty. I managed that before I left Bombay."

Swapna hoped that Anita would get the balance money soon. Harry offered all the help possible.

Used to a luxurious lifestyle, Natasha was bored with the conversation. She took Arjun away to a corner to remind him that he was the only man in her life. At that point, Aneesha butted in, asking him whom he would marry.

"I don't want to get married again. And as dad says, it's not in vogue either," he replied. Everyone burst out laughing.

"I know about you and Natasha," remarked Harry.

"How did you expect him not to know this?" asked Swapna. Everybody laughed.

"Natasha has been broadcasting this. And dad, I did not have the guts to tell you," said Arjun.

"I don't hide anything from you. Do you think I care what you do? Life is just playing musical chairs from one to the other. Flirt with life, the only way out," responded Harry.

"That's great, dad! Like father, like son."

Father and son hugged and everyone was all smiles, except Natasha, who looked quite bored. She pulled Anita away and asked her for a hard kiss.

7
Anita pins down Natasha

Natasha was at her worst behaviour, pulling Anita away from the others and demanding a kiss from her. Anita decided to put an end to her nonsense.

"You are going bonkers, Natasha, control yourself," she said.

"You were eyeing Arjun all the time when he was in his trunks at Calcutta Club. You have blown your gasket. I am going to...."

Anita sealed her lips with hers. She pressed her mouth hard against Natasha's, then jabbed her under-tongue with the tip of her tongue, to settle the score. Being physically stronger, she knew how to control Natasha when required. Natasha got what she wanted and their tongues caressed every nook and corner of each other's mouth. What a tongue twister, thought Anita, as they discreetly re-joined the group.

The discussion going on was about the allocation of rooms to the members of the group. Natasha said she would not share her room with anyone except Anita.

"Fine," said Arjun, *"I will shift to a cosy room next to yours if you help me set it up."*

"Aneesha and I are shifting to a hotel nearby; don't you worry," said Khush.

"Arjun, we will set you up in no time," offered Anita.

"Hold it, I have got the room ready, it doesn't have an independent loo, though," said Swapna.

"That's no problem, there's one common between this room and mine," replied Arjun.

"You are wonderful Swapna, my swapna, my dream. I would be lost without Aneesha and Khush staying with us tonight," added Harry.

Khush heaved a sigh of relief and bowed low to thank Swapna. She had planned it all. Aneesha and Harry were pleased too.

"We have had a long day, so let's have an early night. Dinner will be served in ten minutes," announced Swapna.

"No, not so early," protested Natasha.

"Anyone who wants to eat later can serve themselves. The leftovers will be in the kitchen. Please don't forget to use the dishwasher," said Swapna.

That was that! Ramu was busy setting the table. After dinner, the youngsters went out and the elders settled down in nightwear with their choice of a nightcap. They were all in Harry's master bedroom, adjoining the room where Aneesha and Khush would spend the night.

Swapna was sitting on the couch with her lovely skin showing through her negligee. Khush was seated next to the eye candy.

He wondered what Harry might think, but Swapna aroused his desire. He kept looking for Harry's reaction but found him completely immersed with Aneesha.

Harry didn't seem to worry about what Khush or Swapna thought about it. He was bindaas. Khush felt so guilty that he did not care what Harry and Aneesha were after.

Swapna caught his attention. *"Hey Khush, what's wrong with you. You seemed to be very possessive about Aneesha. Don't worry, Harry will never harm a woman,"* she said, as she drew close and put her hands around him.

The mere sight of her bare armpits was enough to melt Khush.

8
Khush loses control

The next morning there was chaos at Dum Dum airport. Jet Airways cancelled its flights, inconveniencing the entourage flying back to Bombay. Still asleep, Natasha had to be put into the car to take her to the airport to catch an earlier flight.

Fortunately, for Khush, Aneesha, and Swapna, their Air India flight was only in the afternoon. Harry realised that Khush was not his usual self.

"Khush, what's the matter, why are you behaving so strangely?" he enquired.

"Things are out of my control," replied Khush.

"Learn to lose control, become bindaas!"

"You don't want to know what happened between Swapna and me last night."

"Swapna is not the kind to create a problem. And the two of you hit it off well. Then what is the issue?"

"She's your soulmate, I don't want to hurt you."

"I don't think you would do so." Harry led Khush out into the garden.

Swapna and Aneesha were in the bath.

"You seem to have a lot of wrong notions. It's my fault; I have not told you everything. Swapna and I are independent of each other. It took us nearly forty years to get there. The worse thing that can happen to us now is to get into a relationship. You can help us by ensuring that we don't fall into this trap again. I will also be doing you a good turn by giving you someone you love. I remember you telling me what your grandpa did to you when you were 15, with the lovely Parsi widow in Goa. I look so much like him and I did the same thing by taking away Swapna from you when you were fifty and in Bombay. So cheer up and have her now."

"Can you tell me everything that happened between you and Swapna from the time she was fourteen?"

"Of course, I will, though it will be quite a time-consuming exercise."

"You have still not told me about ganja and the bindaas story, and how the two are connected."

"That, I can narrate without you having to miss your flight. Let's go in and see what's taking them so much time in the bath."

Swapna and Aneesha were neither visible in the living hall or the kitchen. Harry and Khush went up to look for them and saw them coming out of the bath together, beaming from ear to ear. On seeing Harry, they were all over him, feeling good because Harry could feel their joy. Khush found Swapna gorgeous with her hair tied up. He was tempted to get into bed with her again, but his thoughts were interrupted by Anita coming up the stairs.

"Did you guys miss your flight?" asked Khush.

"*No only I missed it, the others are on their way back to Bombay,*" she replied.

"*How did you miss it?*" Swapna wanted to know.

9
One for the road

Swapna and Aneesha were not to be seen in the living hall or the kitchen. Anita looked pale and defeated; no one had ever seen her like that. She always exuded confidence and was full of energy.

"Where is your baggage?" asked Swapna.

"In the car. I drove it back. We were supposed to leave it in the parking lot for the driver to bring back."

"And why have you come back?"

"Natasha and I had a big fight in the car, when she finally woke up just before reaching Dum Dum. I forcibly changed her clothes while she was asleep in the car. I packed her belongings too. But when she went through her suitcase, she found one thing missing and she blamed me for it."

Swapna knew what that was, but she kept quiet.

"At the airport she checked in with her handbag, leaving Arjun and me to handle her suitcases. We were already late and the security wouldn't let me check in. My ticket was with Natasha. Arjun and I tried frantically to explain my situation, but the security wouldn't budge. Being election time, they are on high alert."

Anita began to cry. Swapna put an arm around her to pacify her. She was upset with Natasha. Realising that Anita could not have eaten anything since the morning she took her down for breakfast. Anita's situation was quite helpless since she had no job. Later, Swapna brought her to the bedroom and suggested that she rest awhile.

When Swapna returned to the master bedroom to be with Harry, he gave her a questioning look.

"I didn't ask, but you seemed to know what was missing from Natasha's suitcase."

Swapna tried to supress a smile before breaking out into giggles. *"It was the double-headed dildo; Natasha's precious possession. I had taken it away from her room yesterday."*

Both burst out into laughter.

"When you were dancing with Aneesha, I found her too tantalising. I took her up and we felt each other and talked. She was all charged up when I showed her Natasha's double-headed dildo."

"So what did you do?"

"We hugged and kissed. I felt her there. She was extremely sensitive. This morning we did it all and had a bath together."

Harry caressed her smiling lips with his and she clung to him. They went all the way, slowly but surely. Swapna thought this was one for the road for her.

Harry dropped Swapna, Khush, and Aneesha to the airport and ran some errands before going for a swim and dinner at the club. Back home, he hit the bed when Anita knocked on his door.

10

Anita bonds with Harry

Realising that it could only be Anita at the door, Harry sat up and straightened his pyjamas before asking her to enter. She was all dressed up.

"Are you going out or are you back from somewhere?"

"I have been here all day. Just had a bath after a long snooze. I knew you were in, no sooner I heard your air-conditioner running."

"Sorry, I have been a bit unsocial today; I had a lot going on in my mind."

"Not at all. I know that the four of you left immediately after lunch and you have come back only now. I used this opportunity to catch up on my sleep."

"Very nice! When is your flight to Bombay?"

"I want to ask if I can spend some more time here to get my bearings right."

"Suit yourself, I have no problem. Did you eat on time?"

"Yes. Swapna fed me brunch when I came back starving. I just had another meal and I am done for the night. Can I get you something to eat?"

"Glad that you have eaten. I am not a good host and Ramu is away. I had my meals at the club. I can only give you company for a nightcap."

"Wow, thanks. That will be great!"

"I have been recommended pan liqueur as a digestive and for good sleep."

"I would love to try it."

Harry poured the drink into liqueur glasses and sure enough, after a few sips they felt relaxed. Propped up by pillows, he reclined on the bed and she sat on the couch across.

"I don't feel like going to Bombay, I have nothing to do there. I enjoyed my work. It also acted as a workout. But now with the closure, I am all at sea."

"What if you and Natasha team up to start a new venture? She has the money and you are industrious. It will provide you with an occupation and financial stability. And a sense of purpose will give her mental stability."

"It makes sense. I tried to reason it out with her; that's why I am here. She was gung-ho initially, but now everything has backfired; we have had a major rift."

"What about?"

"About Arjun. She suspects I am trying to woo him. This is not true."

"This is typical of Natasha. She is afraid she will lose both, if you and Arjun get together. But in Bombay, the three of you will not be together. It will work out."

"With her, you can never tell. She's too fickle-minded. I like it very much here. Calcutta has had a feel-good effect on me."

"What do you like about this place?"

"Difficult to say. Maybe it's just the British legacy or the people who are arty and intellectual."

"I was born here a year before independence. At that time, it was the second-best city in the world after London. I shifted to Bombay after my schooling, when the Naxalite movement began."

"My grandpa is from here. My dad also studied here, but I was born in Bombay. I have a feeling that my business can grow here."

"I will wait for the election results before I plan anything. I want my birthplace to regain its charm and status."

"That will be lovely, I love this place, Salt Lake City. This house is beautiful, especially the outhouse. The glass walls give you the open-to-sky feeling. I am sure you do your workout there. How else would you have such a trim and fit body?"

"Yes. Today, of course, I went for a swim at the Calcutta Club. But you can use it."

"Thanks, I would love to. I work out when I give stretches and deep tissue massage. You remember the therapy I gave you once? You said you loved it. Do you want it now?"

"I would be happy with a session tomorrow."

"Right! Let's do it tomorrow. Good night!"

Next morning, they woke up to a cocktail of orange juice, lime, and garlic. After breakfast, they headed for the gym in the outhouse. Harry was startled when they met. Anita looked stunning in her racy and come-hither gym gear.

11

Working out with Anita

Harry looked at Anita again; he had never seen her like this before. Oh my God, what is He up to now? He wondered why He couldn't leave him in peace.

Anita admired the scene outside. Open to nature, yet in complete privacy. She turned towards Harry, who was checking her out.

"Why are you looking at me like that?" she enquired.

"I am admiring God's creation, like you are," he replied naughtily.

Anita blushed on seeing his unapologetic desire. But Harry decided not to get carried away; some control was necessary. Beauty was meant to be admired, not grabbed.

"Anyone admiring God's beauty automatically looks admirable," he said.

Anita smiled as she led him by his hand to the gym in the basement. It was equipped with a variety of machines. Harry pulled out a resistance band, his constant companion, and began to demonstrate a range of exercises.

"I don't allow myself an excuse for not having access to a gym or a pool," he added.

"Very impressive, but for today please keep it away as we have to do some cold stretches to warm up. After that we can start off with exercises," she responded.

"What comes first, cardio or weights?"

"The hard and cold stretching to begin with and warm stretching later. The rest can be done in consultation with your trainer."

"Are you going to be my trainer?"

"Only if I can be of help."

"I like that. You will ensure that I get there."

"I want to check your metabolic age and related factors before I make the final plan," said Anita.

She drew closer to Harry and examined him by applying pressure at various points to assess his reactions.

"It's easy to know about your body and mind because you don't conceal anything."

She stood facing him, pushing his palms with hers, and stretching their butts, backs, and hamstrings to the maximum. Then, standing back-to-back, hand in hand, they extended their arms, raising them for a chest stretch. How Harry wished he could see the two of them stretch! He asked her. She nodded and did the arm and shoulder stretches. She could see his chest stretch and when he did the same to her, he noticed how her chest stretched forward exactly the way he had imagined.

"The stretches are over. We must now do cardio or weights. I suggest you do either on alternate days. Beginning next week, do weights and cardio, in that order. The reverse is prone to injury," advised Anita.

"Do I need to increase my muscle mass?"

"Yes, and you must reduce your fat as well. Let's start doing the weights now before the body temperature drops. Let's do this facing the mirror, not facing each other or even looking out through the glass. Fifteen minutes each of heavy weights and strength training. Planks and warm stretches thereafter."

They worked out without uttering a word. After a short break, Harry did his planks, staying in that position for five minutes. Anita was impressed by his stamina. She came on him for the post-workout stretches. They were vigorous, yet loving. Anita identified each exercise by name. Halasana was the sexiest, thought Harry. Afterwards, they lay down exhausted. Anita gave him a glass of fresh lime and water. They had a power nap and showered before Harry left for work. He kissed her on the forehead before setting out.

When he came back after a dinner meeting, Anita was not to be seen. He changed into pyjamas and went to bed when there was a knock on the door. It was Anita in a negligee.

"How about a nightcap?" she asked. Harry was all smiles.

12
Beyond the nightcap

Anita walked in, as if strutting on the ramp, wearing a negligee that came up almost a foot above her knees. She looked like an enchanting seductress from the city of joy.

"Why a nightcap when the night is as beautiful and young as you are? Let me get some bubbly," said Harry.

He produced a Perrier-Jouët Grand Brut, popped it open, and poured it into two glasses.

"Why did you choose to seduce me like this?" asked Harry, unable to take his eyes off her seductive lips moving on the glass rim as they sipped at the bubbles.

"Did you give me a choice? You played so hard to get that I decided not to give you a choice," said Anita.

She moved her face close to his. The warmth of her seductive breath was enough for him to put aside his favourite bubbly and take her glowing cheeks in his palms. His lips felt the flesh of her lusty ones as his mouth took her lower lip. She gripped his upper lip with a slight impression of her teeth and the firmness of her upper lip to close the circuit. Their tongues fenced each other, penetrating and exploring every nook and corner of the other's mouth. He lifted her to the bed and feeling her wet inside, pierced her like a knife in through butter. She came on hard and he was more than a match. They were exhausted by the end of it all. The only energy they had left was enough to collapse on each other. They slept with her head on his chest and his arms enclosing her.

Early in the morning, she tiptoed to her room before Ramu entered the house. When they met for breakfast, they were all smiles. Swapna called to ask Harry about him and Anita. She was thrilled to know that Anita was giving him good company, more so after her own rendezvous with Khush.

"Anita is going to support our cause," said Swapna. *"This has also taught us not to get attached to anyone."*

"Well said. God has his ways to give back what he takes, but with new challenges and excitement. He leaves it to us to make the best of it or otherwise," said Harry, handing over the phone to Anita.

Anita was startled, but she was listening to their conversation keenly, so she took the phone from Harry's hands.

"Hi Swapna, I am taking a good break and absorbing all the learnings from the guru. We had a fabulous workout yesterday. I love this place, but I will decide after the elections are over. Harry and I are returning to Bombay tomorrow," said Anita.

In the outhouse, they lay down on the bed, reliving their fabulous time the night before.

"You are the healthiest man I have ever met. I can tell because I have dealt with them all," said Anita.

"What about my age? You told me that I was fat," asked Harry.

"Your fat mass is a bit above normal but your muscle mass is good. The age to consider is not the number of years you have lived, but the metabolic age."

"What's my metabolic age?"

"We will get it checked at CCI. They have the best machine. It's likely to be around 50. That means you are younger than Khush. But don't get complacent, let's do our workout."

Saying so, Anita rose from the bed, all charged up.

13

Back in Bombay

Harry and Anita were on the flight to Bombay, having worked round the clock to wind up before leaving Calcutta. Harry concluded his discussions with Haldia Refinery and promised to get back to them, after the government formation.

Anita had had discussions with three spa owners in Salt Lake City. Red Rose Spa had expressed interest in her. She had to send them a project report.

"I heard you on the phone. You must progress because you have the calibre. If you don't, we have no business to be together," said Harry.

"You are unnecessarily being harsh on our relationship," replied Anita.

"No relationship! No attachments! Ours is a friendship, which is more like a detached attachment. No strings attached. It is an arrangement that has no name and no rules to follow. It must be a win-win."

"I get the message. If you do not become healthier and fitter than what you are today, I am not required."

"Nice, that was quick," said Harry, kissing her on the cheek.

"Do you love me? You have never said you do," asked Anita.

"Do I need to say that? Love speaks for itself. You can feel it, basic instincts speak for themselves."

"Basic instinct is animal instinct, not love," countered Anita.

"What is love, but purity like instinct? Natural behaviour, not something you have learnt, thought about or planned."

"Survival is the primary instinct. Then comes love, hate, and fear."

"So we know now what love is. A relationship is just a barrier. Relationships are manmade, while love is Godly."

"How can you love both Swapna and me?"

"Why put restrictions on love? Love is limitless. A relationship isn't. You are better off without being in one."

"Did you break up with Swapna?"

"Yes, we did, to cut off our relationship. Our love has stood the test of time."

"But isn't Swapna your soulmate?"

"A soulmate is the means to love, it is the purity within. This resides in every person. Wherever you find it, it is the connection to the soul."

"Can you have more than one soulmate?"

"Why not? There cannot be a singular soulmate because the soul is limitless purity, it is not a person."

"So, are we soulmates?"

"Only if we are free of attachment and it is a win-win."

They looked happy. After their meal, Anita asked for a blanket that she spread on Harry and herself. They tried to take a nap. Suddenly, Harry felt Anita's hand stroking his pubic bone. Much as he wanted to object, he could not. The sensation was pleasing. Anita had the art of feeling the right muscle and applying the right amount of pressure. Harry's expressions seemed to convey that he was enjoying the massage, while wondering what she was up to.

"This is a prostate massage, which every man needs. With age the prostate tends to get enlarged," said Anita, as if reading his mind.

"How do you know so much about me?"

"I know more about men than they do. Just as you know more about women than women do. I will teach you Kegel exercises to strengthen the pelvic floor muscles. This supports the bladder and bowel, and improves sexual function."

"My God, you have taken your job seriously."

"I have to empower myself and others like me."

"Just be careful, it's a man's world. Men feel threatened by women like you."

"You are right. In my profession, I try to learn Sanskrit to enhance my credibility."

"How does that help?"

"A yoga teacher is free to teach exercises and partner-stretching, and work on every muscle in the body, so long as he can define a procedure and give it an appropriate Sanskrit name."

The stewardess announced that they would soon land in Bombay. Anita's thoughts returned to recovering her dues from her ex-employer Mariwala.

Harry turned to Anita and asked, *"Where do you stay?"*

14
Anita in Harry's pad

The moment they landed at Santa Cruz, WhatsApp messages began to pour in. Harry read a long one from Swapna. It said that Anita didn't have a place to stay anymore. Upon Natasha's insistence, she had given up her employer's flat. But after Natasha's outburst, Anita had nowhere to go.

"Where do you stay?" asked Harry.

"With the Mariwalas in Colaba," replied Anita.

Once they had settled in the car, Harry broached the subject.

"You should not be staying with the Mariwalas, unless you want to forego the money that they owe you."

"I don't have any other place to go to."

"Come and stay with me."

"What! Are you sure?"

"You can occupy the room that was Raima's."

"Oh really! You are my God-sent guru," she said and hugged him passionately.

They reached Harry's pad and he showed Anita around. Raima's room was the most spacious one, with a bathroom attached. Anita thought it was too lavish for her. She didn't mind using Harry's room if he would move to Raima's room. But Harry preferred being in his own room. Prakash served them high tea.

"I have not seen such a beautiful view of the sea. This feels like living in it," exclaimed Anita.

"I am glad you like it and I expect you to shift to your own apartment in good time," replied Harry.

"Most certainly. This place motivates me to do my best."

"Please do not give this as your address to any business contact."

"Certainly not! Now please look at me a bit kindly and rest assured I will prove you right."

"I love your charms. I wish I could make a video of your expressions. You have an expressive face."

"How many girls do you want to seduce?"

Harry laughed heartily. "Wherever I find this inner beauty I first saw in Swapna."

"What sort of a man are you?"

"In one word, I am a flirt. I flirt with life."

"A flirt is never attached to anyone."

"Look how Tiger Woods regained his pride. He made a point that we must be honest to ourselves."

She looked at him lovingly. Holding her by the hand, Harry led her to his room.

15
Anita and Natasha hit it off

Harry called Swapna the next day and set up a meeting for Anita and himself. Swapna invited them over to her place. Natasha was there, waiting for them. She came forward to hug Harry and Anita when they arrived and pulling Anita by her hand, led her away.

"They seem to be in love with each other. Natasha's apprehension about Anita falling for Arjun's charms and suspicion about stealing the double-headed dildo appear to have vanished," remarked Swapna.

"That because you owned up to stealing her dildo," said Harry.

"It's you, not Arjun, whom Anita is after."

"Likewise, it's you, not Anita, who stole the dildo," countered Harry in jest. The leg-pulling went on for a while.

"We are so different from others; I feel strange. We don't belong here," commented Swapna.

"We are the liberated ones. Be glad we mingle with everyone. Today, more and more people don't consider sex taboo. It is a basic need, just like food," said Harry.

"Sex is food for both, mind and body."

"And if you call it dirty, your mind, and body would be dirty."

"It is possible to outgrow anything that's not tabooed."

"Because you are no longer attached, you don't end up being possessive or a rapist."

Harry was so pleased with life that he began to flirt with Swapna. He tried to seduce her while she was doubling with laughter. Both were in a jovial mood and making digs at each other. Jumping into bed, they got playful, throwing pillows at each other.

Before they knew it, they were in a physical encounter. Pure to the core, they peaked simultaneously and remained entangled in bed thereafter.

"Anita is a godsend for us," said Swapna.

"Absolutely! She's a breath of fresh air for me, but too involving. It's a challenge to bring about a win-win for everyone and in every possible way," added Harry.

They heard a round of hearty laughter from Natasha's room, and straightened up. Anita entered the room.

"Natasha is coming home to stay with us," announced Anita as she entered the room.

16

All together

"*Hey, Harry,*" said Khush on the phone.

"*How are you doing, Khush?*" asked Harry, while having a nightcap with two beautiful women.

"*Did you read about Ness Wadia being imposed with a 2-year prison sentence in Japan for possession of cannabis?*"

"*Sad! When we ban something, we do not allow anyone to outgrow it. The youth are the victims. We are responsible for misleading them.*"

"*Why is the media silent on such grave issues? The Americans were the ones to ban cannabis for their own gains and the rest of the world followed. Now they have legalised it for its health benefits. But by not legalising it here, smugglers and terrorists stand to gain. The cannabis concentrate capsule they produce is in great demand. The deprived youth here are spending their hard-earned money to fund such people.*"

"*If only more funds were available for vocational training programs in my factories!*"

"You are building an army of trained engineers and highly skilled workmen and helping them secure employment. I know because I keep getting feedback."

"That's a lot you know."

"I get the news from the smart principal you have hired for your CSR activity."

Suddenly, Anita and Natasha jumped up. They looked thrilled at what they saw on their iPhones and showed it to Harry who was equally thrilled. He told Khush to look up the post on his phone. Khush called out to Aneesha who wanted to celebrate this development.

"I can't believe that the UN has eventually declared Masood Azhar a global terrorist," she said in joy. *"It's a proud moment for every Indian. India now has a say on the world stage."*

"This is a major diplomatic win for India," said Harry to Khush. *"Thanks to our dear Shom's mails relaying Saif's correspondence with JEM. This will enhance your clout in official circles."*

Aneesha called Swapna who sounded equally upbeat. She wanted everyone to come over to her place. Eventually, they all met at the Bombay Presidency Golf Club, Chembur the following day. The venue suited Natasha, as Arjun didn't like the place and stayed away, thereby eliminating the possibility of him seeing Anita in her sexy outfit.

Natasha was fine with Harry's closeness to Anita, but Arjun was a different matter.

At the club, Anita clung to Harry and expressed a desire to learn golf. As they were about to enter the walkway adjoining the first hole, she saw Mariwala arguing with his caddy. He noticed her too. Harry slipped away from there to get Khush into the picture.

"What have you done with Anita?" asked Khush.

"She spotted Mariwala on the first tee off and needs your help," said Harry.

Khush went up to Mariwala and enquired, *"When did you take to golf? Are you playing a four–ball, waiting for the others?"*

"No. I am a new member and I was on my way to the other side to shoot some balls. I have been asked by the coach to practice with my clubs," replied Mariwala.

"I see," said Khush looking at his set of old and heavy clubs. *"Better get some graphite ones if you want to get on to the greens and acquire a handicap. This old Wilson set won't do anymore,"* he advised.

"Don't worry, Anita, I will get in touch with you," said Mariwala, shifting his gaze to her.

"When? I need my money immediately," said Anita.

Khush gave Mariwala a questioning look that made the latter nervous.

"I was going to call you to pay you the rest of the money. Please come to the office tomorrow to collect it," he said.

"Let her know the exact time. She now works with Harry and needs to plan her day accordingly," added Khush.

"OK, OK," stammered Mariwala.

Everyone was eagerly waiting for Khush and Anita.

"His tone changed the moment he saw Khush," said Anita, narrating the encounter.

"I guess he didn't want to be exposed in a club full of people who matter," thought Khush.

"Just like my girl," said Natasha and hugged Anita.

"Now is the time to celebrate," summed up Harry.

17
Harry's early years

They had all settled down with their drinks at the bar, overlooking the first and the tenth tee-offs when the news breaking on the television channel surprised them.

Masood Azhar being put on the global terrorist list by UN was welcome, especially in India. Khush showed them a WhatsApp message he had received from the police chief, recalling the efforts of Shom and Raima in nabbing Saif Ali. It was part of the evidence that was sent to China, leading to this development. They were all jubilant and they connected with Anu and Sanjib in Calcutta on Facetime.

"This proves that true lovers like Romeo-Juliet, Laila-Majnu, and Heer-Ranjha needn't have killed themselves," summed up Harry.

"Death was just an escape from the pressure to separate, with the hope of reuniting after death. Attachment matures to true love by living apart with memories and transmuting the energies into positive achievements like Radha-Krishna. True love doesn't have a purpose; it is detached love or detached attachment. Shom and Raima's love was the purest form of it because their souls merged into one another. And generated positivity for the country."

"Now I understand what you and Mom have gone through," commented Natasha. She didn't have the patience to hear about Shom and Raima yet again. She wanted to sit beside her mother, and Swapna reciprocated the feeling.

This was a rare moment. Mother and daughter rarely got along and even for a person like Swapna it was not easy to conquer this attachment. Harry had also gone through this phase. But Arjun and he were more like friends now. Unlike mother and daughter, they gave each other plenty of space. Natasha had grown up with a horrendous father and a protective mother, which had deprived her of freedom and relationships. Shom had aborted the one with Raima and now, she had to share Anita with Harry. Her life was a mess but she was a millionaire. Grandpa had left her all his shares and her father's shares had automatically been transferred to her. Under Swapna's stewardship, the company had grown ten-fold. Much as her mother tried, Natasha refused to work. She was a lost soul, but calculative too.

Though she grudged Harry's role in Anita's life, it also acted as a shield against Arjun's involvement, lest it turn out like that of Shom with Raima. Of late, she had been able to draw Arjun's attention to herself by keeping Anita busy with Harry. This is how her mind worked. Natasha was in a good mood, having spent some quality time with Arjun earlier in the day.

At the same time, she wanted Swapna and Harry to be together for the security of having a fatherly presence around. She teamed up with the others who wanted to know about Harry and Swapna's past.

"You have been cornered, Harry," said Khush, and everyone except Swapna agreed. She was reluctant to talk about her affair with Harry when she was only 15-years-old.

"How old were you at that time?" continued Khush.

"I was only twenty-eight," said Harry.

"The first time we met was when my cousin was at Elphinstone College. We had gone to Samovar Café, at Jahangir Art Gallery, opposite the college. As we entered, I saw a group of young collegians who were football enthusiasts. One stood out in every way. Everyone was addressing him as Harry. They were asking him about the moves the players were making in the match that was being telecast. His face was very expressive. I managed to draw his attention and he felt conscious about it," recalled Swapna.

Harry continued. *"I was there with the St. Xavier's College football team. This was a Mohun Bagan–East Bengal final. How I wished Dilip dada was with me!"*

"All the same, I was not able to ignore this young and appealing girl. Her innocence reminded me of Nancy, the girl from school."

"I had no idea about his football team or where they were from. They left no sooner the match ended, delighted that their team had managed to win. All I could manage was an exchange of glances that stayed with me. I used to think about him, but had no idea of his whereabouts. A year later when I was fifteen, I joined St. Xavier's, where I ran into one of the guys from Harry's group at Samovar in the college canteen. I encountered Harry soon thereafter. I was nervous because he was much senior to me. They were a group of

three boys and two girls who dragged me along to Bullock Carts, the popular club at Kala Ghoda, at that time."

"*What did Harry look like, then?*" asked Natasha.

 "*A younger and better version of Arjun,*" replied Swapna. "*Now let's change this topic.*"

"*Why?*" asked Natasha, and everyone seemed equally curious.

But Swapna wouldn't relent. "*I want to know what Harry was up to, before we met. All I can say that he was my Mills & Boon man, and now he is simply Tom, Dick and Harry.*"

Everyone laughed and Khush nudged Harry to react, which he did with a grin.

"*I know the feeling that Swapna has expressed. The two of us alone understand it. Put simply, we are not attached to each other. Instead, we see each other in many forms. It's the purity, the divinity and the godliness I would see in Mary, Susan, and Jane,*" said Harry.

"*That's lovely! The way you two put it,*" exclaimed Anita.

"*And in the sense, you love each other like never before, but unlike before,*" added Aneesha.

"*True! I used to toss and turn in bed just thinking about him, now I don't at all. I love him, but don't long for him,*" replied Swapna.

"*We are now detached in the sense that our connection has no boundaries. Detached attachment is an attachment that is stretchable beyond boundaries, yet unbreakable,*" explained Harry.

"This is the love guru speaking," commented Khush.

"Now let him tell you about Nancy; he's always talked about her and expects me to believe that I was Nancy in my previous birth. Who knows and who cares! I just know Harry," said Swapna.

"What were you up to, before you met Swapna?" asked Anita.

"You have told us about Cindy and Dilip, but what did you do between the age of ten and twenty-eight? What did you do for a living?" enquired Khush.

Knowing that he was cornered, Harry ordered a fresh round of drinks. *"I was only ten years old, but mature for my age,"* he began. *"Nancy was four years older. She was stunning and had the perfect body. I used to admire her secretly. We were in a missionary school, Our Lady Queen of the Mission. She was an Anglo-Indian."*

"We were together in a school play and would rehearse after class. I used to watch her undress, secretly in the changing room, after the rehearsal. She apparently knew this, but I realised this much later. She would, in fact, entice me by taking her time stripping and inspecting her breasts in front of the mirror."

"Parents and guests used to be invited to the Annual Day function. Ours was the penultimate performance; the last one was a one-act play that would run for over forty minutes."

"After our play, she went to the changing room. Everyone else was busy and the last performers would come back to change only after forty minutes. I assumed the usual position behind the curtain. This time, she caught me, as if she knew exactly where I was."

"I was terrified at first, but she did not raise an alarm. As l tried to explain, she covered my mouth and then started to undress me. We were too young, totally inexperienced, and nervous. We were stark naked before she took charge. She had me sitting on her lap with her breasts pressing against my back. We went on like this for a long time. She enjoyed fiddling with me. As the last act drew to a close, we dressed and left the room."

"That was the last I saw Nancy. Being a co-ed school only until class V; I had to change schools thereafter. By the time I went back to look for her, she was no longer in school. In those days, there was no means to stay in touch. Phones were few and existed only in affluent homes. That was my 'Summer of '42'," concluded Harry.

18

Psyche nite

Harry could do nothing when Nancy vanished from his life. Even Dilip dada was of little help. Memories were all he could cling to, until he landed up with Bumblee, a married but unsatisfied, desirable and desirous woman he learnt to satisfy. The years rolled by, but the memories of Nancy continued to haunt him. He was frustrated for not being able to get any information about her. A gradual exodus of Anglo-Indians occurred that continued for twelve years and more. She could have been anywhere in the world.

He was in a world of his own, when Swapna came to sit beside him. He looked at her in disbelief and she said something that gave him a start. *"You won't even bat an eyelid."*

The first time he heard this phrase was when Nancy had exclaimed, 'Oh my God, you won't even bat an eyelid'. She had said this while inspecting her erect breasts in the mirror. Harry had been staring away at them, without even blinking. He had seen an exposed pair of breasts for the first time.

No one else had told him so. He felt there was a connection between Nancy and Swapna. They were so engrossed with each other that neither felt the presence of anyone else around, despite all eyes being glued on them. Natasha was thrilled to see this, but she dared not utter a word.

Harry straightened up to reason out the possibility of Nancy and Swapna being one. His mind was racing. Nancy could have died young, as there had been no mention of her in the school magazine.

Harry was so engrossed in his thoughts that he blurted out, "So Nancy couldn't have lived long, she must have died before she was even eighteen."

"What is all this about Nancy? Enough of Cindy and Nancy. We want to know about Swapna now. What happened at Bullock Cart? How did the two of you meet?" asked Natasha.

"The 70s were heavily influenced by the Woodstock era, and Bullock Cart, at Kala Ghoda, was the most happening place in town. Students from Xavier's, Sydenham, and Elphinstone, went there for the 11 am jam sessions," said Swapna.

"When I set my eyes on Swapna again, I was reminded of Nancy. I remembered seeing her at Samovar, a year earlier. She had been on my mind since. I cursed myself for checking out such a young girl, but in a year's time, she had matured a lot. I was dancing away to Sugar, Sugar, by The Archies," added Harry.

"Who were you dancing with?" asked Natasha.

"A senior student from Xavier's; I don't remember her name," replied Harry.

"What were you doing in college at the age of twenty-nine?" enquired Khush.

"I was friendly with Dhamu Malkani, Student General Secretary of St. Xavier's College for four consecutive years. I was a footballer from Calcutta and much sought after by their football team," said Harry.

"Dhamu was quite a man. He was a Physical Trainer when I was in St. Xavier's High School. How did you know him?" asked Khush.

"I was studying engineering at MSU, Baroda and lived in Bombay where my dad was transferred from Calcutta. I met Dhamu when I organised a musical event, on the terrace of one of the buildings of Shyam Nivas, at Breach Candy. This was possible thanks to Dhamu, who lived there. The damages were Rs twenty-five per couple; entry was free for single girls. To heighten the impact, I had the tickets designed with a psychedelic look."

"All tickets were sold out and I made good money. Dhamu provided discotheque-like psychedelic lighting, powerful speakers, and the best collection of music on big magnetic tapes. Rhythm and Blues, Soul Jazz and Santana-Soul Sacrifice were big hits. Rodricks was the DJ. There was no mixing equipment that modern-day DJs use."

"It was the first-ever party in India that served marijuana joints. There was no fuss in those days; the stuff was freely available near temples. There were many known faces in SoBo who bought the tickets. Top model and Miss India, Persis Khambatta was there. The famous longhaired hippy, popularly known as Jesus H Christ was also there, dancing with a beautiful blonde. He used to trade in trendy stuff outside Jahangir Art Gallery. That evening, everyone was bindaas."

"How I wished Nancy was with me that night! But alas, she was long dead. I was only twenty-four and in my final year of my college."

Swapna could not control herself. She drew herself close to Harry and kissed him. *"Your Nancy is back,"* she said.

Khush was nervous about his newfound relationship with Swapna. *"You said everyone was bindaas that evening. Did the word exist at that time?"* he asked.

"Of course! We called anyone who was high on pot, bindaas," replied Harry.

"When did you get into bed together for the first time?" enquired Natasha.

That was way too blunt and everyone was amused. Harry just smiled and nodded.

"Life was all paced out in those days. I couldn't just pull her into a corner, plant a kiss to tell her how much I loved her and ask for her mobile number."

"So what did you do?" asked Natasha.

"Towards the end of our first meeting at Bullock Cart, I tapped her shoulder for a dance to the Bigelow Beats, which was very popular in those days. We really rocked together and the crowd cheered us. We decided to meet again. She was only fifteen and I was not willing to rush her. The attachment was mutual, and we couldn't get away, much as we tried, despite the difference in age."

Natasha squeezed herself beside Swapna, almost pushing her into Harry's lap. Everyone was all ears as Harry spoke of their encounter.

19

Harry and Swapna break up

Swapna planted a kiss on Harry's cheek and move out of his lap to give him some space.

"Don't get excited; we didn't have sex the way you guys do nowadays. There were many awkward moments as Harry was reluctant," began Swapna.

"Why?" asked Natasha.

"It would have been easier, had I been a sugar daddy. Not only was I old enough to be her dad, but also a pauper in comparison to her dad, the famous jeweller of Warden Road. She was destined to marry into a wealthy family as per the norms of society. All our physical encounters were full of guilt," said Harry.

"But we have overcome all the differences now. Our love is like never before, but not like before," added Swapna.

"Our love is bindaas," said Harry.

"What kind of love is this? Did you have sex?" asked Natasha.

"Yes," affirmed Swapna.

"Did you enjoy it?"

"Immensely!"

"*Absolutely. The after-effects were killing. We had to sober down,*" added Harry.

"*Every time we decided to meet, we had to be very cautious,*" said Swapna.

"*Her dad was the suspicious type. It affected my work too. We had to break up,*" said Harry.

"*What nonsense! Why did you have to break up?*" asked Natasha.

"*Because of Nancy,*" said Swapna.

Everyone was taken by surprise. Swapna burst out laughing. Unable to control herself, she walked out of the room. The others turned to Harry for an answer.

Harry obliged. "*It was the tenth year of our relationship; she was twenty-four and I was Thirty-eight. I told Swapna that it was high time she got married. To make sure she moved on, I told her that l was going to marry within a month. We decided to meet one last time at our usual rendezvous. This meeting would stay with us for a lifetime. The meeting took us to new pinnacles. When we were finally exhausted, I called out to Nancy, without realising it. I cannot forget the look on Swapna face.*"

"*She wanted to know who Nancy was. I tried to explain, but she cut me short, accusing me of cheating on her. I had no answer, I had never had sex with Nancy, but she had always been with me. Swapna dressed up and walked off. I joined her at the cafe nearby and ordered two cups of coffee.*"

"We sat across each other in total silence. Slowly, we picked up a conversation, but the more we talked, the less we seemed to say. We were completely out of synch; our thoughts were poles apart. We didn't even look at each. Although done with our usual coffee, neither of us chose to get up from our chairs. We were sitting in a restaurant that was almost empty. Although running a company, I was just an engineer, not a businessman. I had more on my plate than I could chew. She had to rush back, as her dad was keeping a close watch on her. Yet neither of us made the first move; we kept looking everywhere else but at each other, thinking of something appropriate to say before we left. The question was, who would initiate the breakup and how? I knew that after ten years; this was going to be rather tough. Being much older, I had to take this call. I wanted it to be as smooth as possible, so that we remained friends," said Harry.

"I was relieved that she broke the ice by asking me what I was thinking. I said the best we could do was not be dependent on each other, as dependence would degrade our love to the level of attachment. True love was not confined to a single relationship. Separating would protect her dad from the shock of knowing about us. We would demonstrate our strength by going our separate ways."

"A long pause followed. She looked away, staring at the ceiling and I waited for eye contact. Eventually, she looked at me and said that we should leave. I nodded. She seemed to be calm, poised, and not worked up as usual. This was the best thing that could have happened, as I did not want to call it off with sorrow or anger. She turned to face me; an unintended smile appeared on her lips. We looked into each other's eyes, as if looking into our souls."

"It was a spiritual encounter. This was the endorsement we needed to give ourselves confidence. We hugged like never before and parted, telling each other that a break-up could only happen in a relationship, not in love," concluded Harry.

20
Shamiq and his Goddess

"I have been looking for you for years; I had to find you. You are my goddess," said Shamiq.

"What rubbish! I was only sixteen and desperate to have sex; I had to arouse you. I struggled to extract some action out of you," replied Anita.

"You aroused me and how! Oh my God! You are my goddess! That was my first time with a woman. I am otherwise only with the Lord himself."

"You are a freak. Get out of here." Her scream brought Harry into the room.

"What's the matter? Why are you screaming? Shamiq, when did you come?" asked Harry.

"I have been trying to reach her for a long time," said Shamiq.

"How do you guys know each other?" asked Harry.

Anita made a face and charged out, banging the door shut. Harry called Khush and asked him to come there, as Shamiq was around. Shamiq was thrilled as Khush and he got along well. He had located Aneesha and had helped Shom and her in Jaipur. He excused himself and went to the toilet. Stripping, he inspected every part of his body in the full-length mirror.

He was in love with himself. He kissed his reflection in the mirror right on the lips. Then he massaged his groin with body lotion, fantasising about his goddess Anita, and the way she aroused him. Merely seeing her angry was enough to give him a high.

There was a knock on the door. It was Khush with Aneesha beside him. He reached out for her and they hugged like old buddies.

"Please feel at home and help yourself to drinks and something to nibble. Anita has taken Raima's place in the house. I don't know what's happened to her today. Can someone help?" asked Harry.

"I can," offered Shamiq.

"You keep out of it Shamiq, you are the cause."

"Only you can handle her, Harry," said Khush.

Harry knocked on Anita's door. She pulled him in and locked the door. Before he could speak, she stopped him.

"I don't want to socialise today; not with that creep in the house," she said.

"There's nothing wrong with him, he's just gay," said Harry.

"I left Natasha to be with you today, but you don't even look at me nowadays. You are surrounded by people."

"You just relax. I will make an excuse for you and later we will have dinner together; just the two of us."

Anita liked that and she pulled him forward for a succulent kiss that took the breath out of him. He quickly wiped his lips, stroked her cheeks lovingly, and left.

"I see there's a problem," remarked Khush and Harry nodded.

"It's all to do with me," said Shamiq. *"I have been looking out for her because she's the only woman I have had sex with. She's the only one who could arouse me."*

Aneesha patted his back to quieten him; they were similar in many ways. If absolute male and female were the two extremes, *ardhanari* would be the golden mean. They would be closer to the centre, but on opposite sides, Aneesha on the female side and Shamiq, male.

"Shamiq, you have some female biological traits and I have some male. I underwent a sex change," said Aneesha.

"Did you have a prostate gland, which you had removed?" asked Harry.

"I have a prostate gland because I had a penis. The penis and testicles have been removed but not the prostate gland. The clitoris was created from the gland and the head of the penis. The skin on the penis and scrotum was used to create the inner and outer labia," replied Aneesha.

"She has the prettiest outie going. It's very sensitive we are about to locate the G spot," added Khush.

"Hey, you have two G spots; one through the anus and another through the vagina. Give me five!" said Shamiq. *"But I will never*

get my goddess back. I will have to live with my G spot in the prostate with anal pleasure, and never satisfy a female."

"Don't worry Shamiq. I will be your goddess and you can serve me by looking for my new G spot," said Aneesha.

"At your service, my goddess," he said, kneeling before a smiling Aneesha.

21
A goddess in action

"*You forget all about me, when you're with friends,*" complained Anita.

"*I was trying to wind up early, but Shamiq and Aneesha were wondering why a woman with a penis is called a she-male, but a man with breasts is not called a he-female. If a she-male has a prostate gland, how will a gender change from female to male generate a prostate gland?*" replied Harry.

"*What's happened with you tonight, in the company of two transgenders? Please return to your senses. Let's quickly have something to eat; I can give you mutton biryani with raita in a jiffy. It's in the fridge.*"

"*Nice girl. I love you.*"

"*Stop saying things for effect!*"

Anita got busy in the kitchen and Harry laid the table, as Prakash was on leave. They enjoyed the meal. Anita and Harry went for a walk on the stretch between the sea on one side and the woods on the other.

They chewed paan, an after-dinner digestive, a mouth fresher (like mint), a cooling agent, rich in calcium, alkaline, and an antibiotic. They talked about liberated sex and G-spots in men and women. Harry shared his life experiences about how Swapna had always been his strength. Then he told her how Aneesha had become Shamiq's new goddess. Soon, it was time to get back.

Lying in bed, Harry had just finished chatting with Swapna on WhatsApp and was about to switch off his bed lights, when Anita knocked on his bedroom door. She looked irresistible in what she wore, or rather, in what she did not wear.

"I know you are tired I want to give you some goodnight stretches, good for deep sleep," she said.

As she stretched herself on Harry, his smile broadened. He lapped up Anita's love as she stretched every limb in his body. This went on with much sighing, especially during the reverse backstretch. Lying on his abdomen, Harry was made to raise his head and feet, pointing them to the ceiling. Assuming the dhanurasana (bow pose), his hands gripped his legs such that his abdomen supported his entire body weight. She did not allow him to get away without holding on to the posture for five minutes at a stretch. She stood on the bed like a guard, to support his body weight when he held on to her in his failed attempts. When he finally succeeded, he just collapsed. Gasping for breath, he took a break with his nightcap Crema De Cacao and broke into an old comical song.

I married a female wrestler

As massive as can be

She had bulging muscles

Which quite fascinated me.

She said she loved me truly

She also said by heck

If I ever catch you fooling around

I'll break your loving neck.

Ay ay yo, what shall I do?

How shall I save my skin?

I have married a female wrestler

Now look at the mess I'm in.

Ay ay yo, what shall I do?

Harry laughed, but Anita didn't think it was funny; she just took the glass from his hand and gulped it up, with a bottoms up. He looked at her as a goddess. If not Shamiq, then why not him, he thought.

As Anita made him lie on his back and went on to arouse his sleeping giant, Harry took a back seat for once and imagined himself to be Shamiq. His goddess was in action and how! She pleasured his body with her tongue.

She was on top of him, and slowly, he was inside her. The way she did it was so effortless that he realised only when he felt the warmth enclosing his. Then he saw an unusual glow on her face as she continued to transport him to paradise. He was mesmerised, just watching her expressions change as she reached her emotional culmination.

Oh my God, he wondered. The Divinity on her face was something he had never seen before. She was not Anita; she was his goddess. When she saw him looking at her, she lowered her face to his chest in coyness, to escape his glare. She went off to sleep and he embraced her body to imbibe all her godliness. His own paradise remained inside her, assuming the shape of a bow now, slowly receding with a sensation of immense pleasure he had never experienced before. This feeling intensified as the receding went through several layers. Both quivered with intense sensation. Finally, both moaned as it came out of her like a cork popping out of a bottle of champagne. This led to an intense sexual arousal in both. Now it was Harry's turn to serve his goddess. He pinned her down with one pinnacle after other, until they were completely submerged in each other.

22

The morning after

Harry and Anita woke up in the morning facing each other. Anita reciprocated Harry's smile as they remembered the previous night.

Anita got out of bed to begin her workout and chores. Harry was still in a world of his own, thinking about the night before and wondering why he saw the goddess in Anita that he hadn't seen in Swapna, years ago. He realised that the love Swapna and he made was never guilt-free, therefore not worthy of such purity. With Anita, it was different. With no attachment, there was no guilt.

He went back to the night before. Anita had reached her zenith without him getting there. Her pleasure was so intense that he was mesmerised by her expression. Drained with exhaustion, she collapsed on him, enclosed in his arms, her head buried in his chest. She was asleep with him inside her, assuming the shape of a bow. Although he was not done, he felt heavenly because he had given her this joy. Was this not salvation, he wondered.

Furthermore, the pleasure of his manhood receding was one he had never experienced before. Enjoying his sacrifice was salvation indeed, he realised, answering his own question.

On hearing Anita's footsteps, he quickly ran to the toilet with the glass of untouched orange juice that Anita had placed on his side table a while earlier. Anita knocked on the bathroom door to let him know that he would be late for work, unless he completed his workout in 30 minutes flat. Harry rushed through his chores and skipped breakfast to make it in time for his first meeting.

Harry was indeed blessed, revealed the smile on the chauffer's face, as he saw Anita feeding Harry, in the rear-view mirror.

After dropping Harry at his office in Ballard Estate, Anita went off to see Natasha. With Mariwala having fully cleared her dues, together with the comfort of living with Harry, her mind was racing with ideas.

It wasn't the same for Harry. Being much younger and aggressive, Anita stuck to her mission of keeping him on his toes, or rather making him touch his toes, without bending his knees. Harry could impress Anita only with his planks; on other fronts, he had a long way to go. To give her more time, he had no option, but to stop his yoga sessions.

Why be limited to yoga when you can do extensive stretching exercises with a help of therapist like Anita, he thought. Moreover, meditation isolated negativity and disciplined the mind to stay focussed.

Suddenly Harry's phone rang. It was Anita enquiring about his lunch. Prakash being away, she would have to prepare it.

"You treated me like a queen last night. I have never felt like that, this was by far the best," she gushed.

"You are my Queen of Sheeba," replied Harry.

"Is Sheeba a place?"

"Yes, in my heart!" said Harry laughingly and Anita joined in.

"I tried to get up and return to my room but couldn't after the double dose."

"Why would you go? I love to cuddle and sleep."

"What you did to me was unbelievable. I was in heaven. You gave me such a massage. Oh my God! You are a wizard! I just went off to sleep."

"You have done it for me so many times, what I did was learnt from you."

Before Anita could reply, Harry heard Natasha's voice in the background. It was time to get back to work. He had never known Anita to be so emotional; she probably would not have allowed herself to be so in person as that would be too revealing. Harry was moved.

Giving a massage to a masseuse is a service to God, he thought. Bliss can only be reached after salvation. Bliss is salvation.

23
Testing times

Harry was still in his office. The day was ending and the staff was winding up. He looked up to see a familiar frame. It was Khush, the only person who could walk into his cabin without permission.

Harry was glad to see him, but not the way he looked.

"What's the matter, why so depressed?" he enquired.

"The country is coming to a grinding halt, even NaMo supporters are worried now," replied Khush.

"Yes, it's a change, a drastic one, but for the better."

"How?"

"He's a modern-day Robin Hood."

"All the big industrialists are panicking. Every second company is closing down. How's that good?"

"If the middle class and the poor prosper at the cost of the middlemen who pocket all the money, the economy is going to boom."

"Really?"

"If a handful of people make money and spend most of it buying from Amazon or abroad is converted to the buying power of millions of farmers, workers, artists and entrepreneurs, the buying power will rise manifold."

"What are you trying to say when all of us including you are suffering?"

"This is the most difficult phase. We have suffered because the banks have cut off our non-fund and funding limits. Most of the private clients have become NPAs and have invoked advance bank guarantees. Many of our orders are on hold. Yet, I am relaxed because this is a small sacrifice for the nation. Our youth will be proud of their country in the days to come. The young generation may truly be rid of the white skin complex the country has. They will not suffer as we did when we were young."

"You have a way with your thoughts to make him look good. What about denouncing other religions and talking about throwing out the minorities from the country? What about banning cow meat?"

"I agree, no one has the authority to dictate one's eating habits. What to eat should be decided by the consumer and not by the authorities who prohibit the sale for their agenda. I earnestly hope he corrects this along with other things that are banned. Let's step out. The times they are 'a-changin', let's change with the times, the early birds will enjoy the happy hours!" said Harry.

They stepped into the Clearing House lounge, at walking distance from his office and settled down with a drink.

"Where's Aneesha?" asked Harry.

"Getting along well with Shamiq," replied Khush.

"And Swapna, where is she?"

"I thought I would meet you before I meet her."

"Why you want my permission?"

"Because you love each other."

"No! Love is not about each other, relationships are."

"Of course, you do, and she does too."

"Love is independent, devoid of relationship, how can it be with each other?"

"What crap is that? Love is not with each other, who's going to believe that?"

"Love is between the souls, not between individuals. That's a relationship."

"Don't you guys make love even now?"

"Yes! We do and it's bliss. This is a detached attachment. Where we discover and love our own self more and more. The relationship is not between us but between our souls. We are trying to possess ourselves and not each other. Love is free, love is freedom!"

"This is completely beyond me. All I can see is you are a completely liberated man and so is she."

"No! Honestly, I am only trying to get there; it's a path to enjoy your salvation. What you were asking me were indeed burning questions that I ask myself and when I get the answers, it is bliss."

"Where is Anita?"

"With Natasha. We are in the same boat."

Just then, there was a call on Harry's phone. It was Swapna. Khush's eyes popped open.

24
Aneesha and Shamiq's double-headed joy

Harry's phone buzzed. Swapna was on the line. Khush was surprised. He was about to rise to leave the room when Harry activated the speaker.

"Is Khush with you?" asked Swapna.

Harry laughed aloud and said, *"Yes, and he won't believe that you called me to enquire about him."*

Khush fished out his phone, only to curse himself when he saw that there were several calls from Swapna he had missed because his phone was on silent mode. Harry handed him over his phone.

"Hello, Khush! Aneesha tells me that she is getting together with Shamiq. Why didn't you tell me? Please come home; I'm waiting for you."

Khush was thrilled, but felt awkward. Harry immediately called Anita for a dinner date.

As Harry and Khush went down to their respective cars, Harry's thoughts travelled to Aneesha and Shamiq, and their long-awaited adventure.

- - - - -

"What are you up to, Shamiq?" asked Aneesha.

"Nothing in particular," replied Shamiq. *"When can we meet?"*

"Today!"

"Wonderful! You have been featuring in my fantasies."

"I love the way you talk, Shamiq! I'm at home. Come over anytime you want."

Shamiq rushed out to be with her, in his brother-in-law's sprawling apartment at Dalamal Towers, one floor below his own apartment. He ran down the steps, rang the doorbell and voila! Dressed in nothing but her briefs, Aneesha opened the door.

"No one's here. I have some joints rolled up and ready," she said.

"Where's my bro?"

"With Harry; he knows we're together."

"My guru. I'm a kid in comparison, only slightly older than Anita."

Aneesha pulled him up close and gave him a voluptuous kiss that left him gasping for breath. She lay him down on the bed. *"Don't talk about that bitch."*

"She's a bitch all right, we'll get even with her," he said, going for Aneesha's juicy armpits. He sucked them out and she was in heaven. His tongue was longer and stronger than his dick. He

licked every part of her body; every bit was sensational. Her body was on fire and that in turn fired up his tongue further.

He went for her lips - the ones hidden under her panties. The outies looked enticing. They assumed a 69-position with Aneesha on top, struggling to arouse his, while his tongue went through all the layers from the tip of the cervix to the depth of her vagina and he sucked her inside out.

Aneesha moaned as she exclaimed, *"There is no single G-spot, we have multiple ones, and you have just made me experience that. The clit of course is the most pronounced one."*

"Yeah, that was great for me too and now I'll go for your male G-spot," he said, as he put his fingers though her rectum.

His fingers in the rectum and tongue in the vagina were separated only by a thin membrane. The fingers probed deeper to press her prostate against his tongue. Aneesha screamed with pleasure. This was a rare combination of two unusual souls locked in an unconventional encounter. A paradise reserved for God's favourite. Shamiq got a hard on inside her mouth. Before they climaxed, they quickly changed their positions, being in total harmony with each other. Aneesha on top lowered herself to his and both of them rapidly stroked each other and climaxed together. His tiny one was larger than ever before. It regressed and withdrew gradually with multiple sensations. Shamiq was experiencing the time of his life.

"Oh my God, what a sensation!" he exclaimed. *"This is how a dog and a bitch continue their pleasure."*

"What has woman on top to do with a dog and a bitch?"

"Dogs make the most of the prolonged regression but we make fun of them."

They fell asleep in each other's arms. When they awoke, Shamiq remembered the joint Aneesha had mentioned earlier. Soon they were merrily smoking up.

"I love you as my younger brother."

"Why not, in our community we don't use derogatory terms such as incest, we're too bindaas."

"I have planned something for us," said Aneesha mischievously.

"What?"

"I wondered why shouldn't a double-headed dildo be designed for use by both genders and got one for us."

"Yes! Why not?"

"I got this one made to order. Here we are," she said as she pulled out the packet. *"From Philadelphia's best sex shop 'The Velvet Lily'. I placed the order the day we first met."*

"You're my goddess, not Anita. She just took me for a ride."

"Forget about her. I'm your elder sister, I will protect you from her. I got this for your G-spot, like you did for mine, now we'll do it to each other."

They went through the instruction manual, excited to see photos of two men; their rectums engaged with the double-header.

25

Memories of another day

Approaching Nepean Sea Road to meet Swapna, Khush recalled the time twelve years ago, when he took up an honorary assignment, as Deputy Chief of the Bomb Squad in the days following 26/11. The squad was summoned early one morning after having worked through the night maintaining vigilance. An explosion had occurred, followed by a continuous earth-shattering sound. The residents of the upmarket area were panic-stricken. The police and the fire brigade were already there when the Bomb Squad arrived. Khush walked past the police cordon and saw an empty steel bin from which the bone-shattering sound emanated. It spelt danger, or worse, death.

Clad in titanium alloy armour and using a long pole, the Bomb Squad tipped the bin over with a forceful jab. A rod-like object sprung out, kicking up dust around where it fell on the ground. Whirring with vibration, it flipped and tossed about in a dance for everyone to see.

The Chief of the Bomb Squad looked thoroughly perplexed.

"What on earth is this gadget?" he asked.

Someone from the crowd was heard saying, *"Looks like a dancing snake."*

The crowd broke out in laughter. The chief cautiously inched towards the vibrating item, while the people peeping from windows came out in their balconies, watching the drama unfold below. This was when Khush side-stepped the chief and grabbed the vibrating rod. He picked it up for everyone to see and switched it off. The smile on his face said it all.

It appeared as though he was defusing a bomb. What followed was a huge applause. He was a hero! The ever-present news reporters and the camera flashers who were in their element post-26/11, made Khush instantly famous.

Khush was beaming with pride and looking at people applauding from their balconies. His eyes were constantly in search of the owner of the tool, not as a bomb squad man for disturbing the peace, but in his personal capacity to oblige the damsel in distress. This was his second nature. He conducted his search and when he eventually landed in the apartment, he could tell from his years of experience that the tool belonged to Swapna.

Raima tried to protect Swapna by claiming to be the owner. Swapna gave him the cold shoulder; it was the first time in his life that a woman had rejected him. He was depressed, but Raima being younger, sexier and eager, was fair compensation. This was before Raima had met Shom, and Khush had no idea of Harry's existence; leave alone the fact that Harry and Swapna had been soulmates in the past.

Khush's thoughts brought him back to the present as he stood in front of Swapna's apartment door after twelve years. She answered the doorbell. Seeing her in an inviting mood, he lifted her off her feet and took her to the luxurious bed in her private chamber.

26
Blow hot, blow cold

As he lay her down on the bed, she held on to him and pulled him down on herself. It was a test of his reflexes to buffer his fall and make a soft landing on her. His face landed softly on her exposed cleavage, which reacted to his warm breath, enticing her to no limits. Slowly, the tip of his tongue moved around her areola, making her sigh and moan deeply, as Khush kept moving it around. Swapna was completely afire and she led him inside her. Khush had never known her to be so aggressive and was exhausted by the time they were done.

"You're my saviour, like Anita is for Harry. You will help my connection with Harry from going back to a relationship," said Swapna.

"You and Harry speak the same lingo, it's all beyond me. We're just satisfying our urges, why think beyond that?" countered Khush.

The loud banging of the door startled them. It was Natasha. They jumped out of bed. Swapna wore her gown and screamed at Natasha. Stepping out of the room, she pushed Natasha aside and shut the door to give Khush the much-needed time. She led Natasha into the hall.

Natasha exploded. *"If Harry is with you, why did Anita ditch me? She told me she had a date with Harry. Why did that bitch lie?"* she screamed.

"Harry is not here. If he was, he would have set you right," replied Swapna.

"Then who's with you? No man has ever come to this house before. How dare you get someone here?"

"I can do as I please. Keep yourself to your bedroom; don't even come to this part of the house."

"Why not? This is my house, not yours."

"You are only a part-owner and I can buy you off for very little. Property prices have crashed."

"I'll buy you off from my shares in the company."

"Unfortunately, your shares have very little value. Your dad was a drunken rotter; he blew up all the money. I had to work hard and get this house out of mortgage and bring you up single-handedly."

"How do we have so much money?"

"Harry's company has contracted its logistics to our company. That keeps us afloat. I'm glad you're asking me so many questions. I have been wanting you to take some interest."

Natasha burst out crying. *"Are we so badly off?"*

"*No, my child, we're not, but you can help the company grow. After I'm gone, you'll have to make the company grow and make you mother and grandpa proud.*"

"*I'll make you proud, Ma,*" she said, hugging her mom.

"*I'm sure you will,*" replied Swapna, reciprocating the hug.

Swapna wondered if she was too harsh on her daughter. But this seemed to be the only way to make her daughter independent. Her own father was ninety, and pressing her to take charge of his business. Natasha cooled down and all was well between mother and daughter again.

Khush came out of the bedroom, all ready to go. "*Is everything all right between the two of you?*" he asked.

27
Women in Distress

Khush stepped out, all ready to go. *"Is everything all right between the two of you?"* he enquired.

"Oh, so it was you in the room with Mom," remarked Natasha.

"Why would I allow you to infringe on someone's privacy?" said Swapna.

"This means Harry has ditched you and you have had to hire a Don Juan for yourself," countered Natasha.

"What!"

"Don't worry, Ma, you're doing the right thing. I do the same when Anita ditches me."

"So you're calling me names? Yes, I agree, but I don't do it for money. I enjoy it when my partners need me. Especially women in distress," said Khush.

"That explains it well, Khush! I need you to save me from my craving for Harry. I have to get rid of the attachment. You are helping me like Anita is helping Harry."

"Harry is ditching you," repeated Natasha.

"No, my child, no one's ditching anyone, we don't believe in relationships, they are not trendy anymore. The trend among women today is to go for variety, exactly like men do."

"Wow! I have never heard that before," said Khush.

"Gender equality," said Swapna.

"Yes, Mom, even I like variety."

"Ah, yes, we know that," said Khush.

"Please keep your opinions to yourself, this is between mother and daughter," said Natasha.

"Okay. I must hurry. There's no time to get into the same old arguments with you."

Khush planted a quick kiss on Swapna's cheek and hurried off to the elevator. He was thinking about Aneesha and Shamiq. It was already past midnight and hopefully they'd be in bed before he returned.

He opened the door and to his surprise, they were right there, on either side of the hallway floor, completely exhausted. A funny-looking object lay close by; it was a double-headed tool. Khush smiled and looked at them again. They were unaware of their surroundings, as if they had passed out. His smile grew into a big grin as he walked into his room.

28

Howdy, Houston!

"Howdy, Harry," said Khush.

"On top of the world," said Harry, with a wide grin. *"Many misguided Indians are coming to their senses."*

"What do you think is happening with our leader?"

"He's in bliss, enjoying his work. He's on a 'Proud Indian' mission. Completely focussed, despite his detractors in the country and elsewhere."

"What's happening in Houston is an unforgettable celebration of the crowning of our leader as a world statesman,' so says a distinguished civil servant," said Khush, quoting from a newspaper.

"Our leader is a strategist of the highest order, knowing well that the President, who's eyeing a second tenure, would not stay away from a 50,000-strong rally in Houston. I have heard great speakers all over the world, but our leader takes the cake."

"How does it help the country?"

"He has sent a strong message to our enemy."

"What about the economy and business prospects?"

"We are buying more than we sell, so we have to increase exports to stabilise our economy. USA is cash-rich; let's give them what they don't have."

"What do they want from us?"

"They'll want to replace China with India as we're a lesser threat."

"That works for both sides."

"You said it!" said Harry, ordering his omelette after a game of tennis at the CCI. Khush followed suit.

Harry's phone buzzed. It was Natasha on the line. Harry put the call on the speaker.

"Harry! I want your permission to go to Houston with Arjun," she said.

"You are an adult. Why do you need my permission?"

"Ma told me to seek your blessings."

"Blessings for what?"

"To study Business Management there."

"Why Houston, of all the places in the US?"

"I have two of my friends from JJ School of Architecture working there. Raima and I had planned to go there too, but Shom took her away like you've taken away Anita from me."

"I have not taken her away; just given her a place to stay, as I did with Raima. In fact, I brought back Raima and Anita for you. Raima

got busy with her work and now Anita is busy with hers. She and I have occasional dates, that's all."

"Now that I have learnt a lesson, I want to do something for myself."

"You're on the right path and you have my blessings."

Khush, who was keenly listening to the conversation, was all smiles.

"I wonder if this is Arjun or Swapna's doing."

Khush told him how Swapna had taken charge of the situation when Natasha had charged in to catch him and Swapna red-handed.

29
Tequila dinner

Arjun and Natasha were outside Picos, Arjun's favourite restaurant in Houston – the Oil & Gas capital of the world.

Harry's technology had made inroads into oil majors such as Chevron, Flour, Exxon, Mobil, ConocoPhillips and KBR in Texas. With the rupee depreciating against the dollar, catering to the export market was the best way forward.

Arjun had cut a smart deal by booking a suite on a monthly tariff at the Houstonian Hotel, Club & Spa.

This time he'd brought Natasha along. They'd already spent a weekend here. Natasha was all praise for the place. She loved the lifestyle there and loathed staying in India. Arjun promised her that it was only a question of time before India was at the top, like the US. This, however, was his wishful thinking influenced by Harry's dreams.

However, at this moment they were in a great mood after the hard work they had put in their respective fields. They were celebrating Natasha's enrolment in the prestigious Johns Hopkins University for an MBA.

Picos, known for their Shaker Margarita, made with the perfect blend of ingredients was the best place to start.

"Ma was so happy today when I gave her the news. Harry was with her. He complimented me and enquired about you," said Natasha.

"I called to let him know that I have made progress with the companies I have met and will keep him updated of developments. I guess both of them are happy. And so, what next?"

"Let's go back to our paradise."

"Yeah, let's have dinner."

"Here or at the hotel?"

"This place is good for Mexican cuisine."

"Let's eat here."

"Okay. How about Tequila Dinners; tequilas with classic Mexican cuisine?"

"Lovely! Let's try it out."

They had a roaring conversation over a hearty meal. On the way back to the hotel, they were eager to get into bed.

"Why have you been keeping away from me?" asked Natasha.

"You are a self-sufficient person. Do you need anyone in your life?" replied Arjun.

"What do you mean? Don't we all have needs?" she continued, noticing Arjun grin.

"Yes, and this place is full of toy shops. You can get anything you want."

"You're such a wicked man! You'll be gone soon, leaving me alone."

"I'll keep coming back as the business grows. Feel free to use my suite; it's booked for six months."

"Thanks, honey. I'll be staying in the university dorm but I'll keep coming here when I want privacy with a friend. And where do I buy my toy?"

"At Pleasure Palace, next to the hotel. What size are you are looking for?"

"The same size as yours. Best suited to me."

They laughed and hugged. Once outside their room, Arjun unlatched the door and both quickly stripped themselves before jumping into the welcoming bed.

30
Garba nights at Radio Club

They were all at the Bombay Presidency Radio Club in Colaba. The club acquired its name from India's first radio station, which began broadcasting from the club in July 1923.

Harry had invited them for the Navratri celebrations on the pier. Couples dancing to Gujarati folk tunes while sword fencing with sticks, gave Anu and Sanjib a taste of Navratri, in lieu of the Durga Puja festivities in Calcutta they had foregone to be in Bombay. They were here because Anu had to take custody of Raima's apartment and take over her fixed deposits with HDFC Bank.

"What are we going to do with the money?" asked Sanjib.

"Why not invest in a start-up? Corporate tax has been reduced," suggested Harry.

"I have been thinking on those lines. I left my lucrative job in the US to start a business, but Calcutta is not the place," replied Sanjib.

"Let's do it in Bombay. We have a beautiful house here, and Raima's memories to keep us going," said Anu.

"I would think so. And as Calcutta regains its past glory, you can start a new vertical there too," added Harry.

"I would love that to happen," said Sanjib.

Loud music took over as Swapna, Anita and Khush joined the party. Natasha, known to be an entertainer for being on a short fuse, was much missed. Nevertheless, the blast of music stirred them up. Garba had commenced! In a wide circle, young men and women dressed in colourful traditional attire were dancing in a form that originated in Gujarati folk dance. An idol of Goddess Durga stood at the centre of the circle. The dance picked tempo as the music changed to *'Dholi taro dhol baaje'*. This was the only time of the year when the club served liquor out in the open.

Although Navratri and Durga Puja are celebrated on the same nine days, the rituals differ from each other. Navratri ends with Dussehra, the final day of Ram Lila, and recalls Lord Ram's victory over *Ravana*. Durga Puja begins with *Mahalaya*, the day when the battle between Goddess Durga and the buffalo demon *Mahishasura* commences. The festivities conclude with the killing of *Mahishasura* on the tenth day. In other parts of India, the tenth day is also celebrated as *Vijaya Dashmi*.

Swapna also urged Anu to shift to Bombay. The two got along well.

"With work opportunities having dried up, Calcutta isn't the city it used to be. Of course, we have our saving to keep us going," remarked Sanjib.

"Bombay is the right place for you. Besides, I'm close to Worli, where you'll be staying. That's where my office is too," added Swapna.

Anu and Sanjib were pulled in for garba. They were hesitant, but Anita urged them into the act and she pulled Harry along. Khush and Swapna joined in too. Anita looked slick in a trendy jacket, long enough to be a mini skirt, and stilettos. Khush looked quite awkward dancing and did not manage to get the steps right. They had a hearty laugh as *'Nagada sang dhol'* played out and rushed to the bar on the first floor with an uninterrupted 180 degrees view of the sea.

Salvation in discomfort

When Shamiq was called upon to perform as a DJ for garba night at Aer bar, he got Aneesha a job as a bargirl. She mixed some amazing drinks, swaying to the music that Shamiq spun away for the audience. The crowd went insane as the music heated up the cool breeze on the 34th floor rooftop. With an amazing view of the city, Aer was one of the fanciest bars in town. Both, Shamiq and Aneesha had admirers wooing them all night.

When they eventually stepped into their room in the early hours, it was twilight. Shamiq collapsed on the bed and lying on his back with his eyes closed, he waited for Aneesha to make the first move. The next moment, he felt her butt close to his face and her mouth coming down on his. The sensation made him grab her kitty in his mouth. His mouth covered her entire slit from her clit to the last orifice and she moaned.

Being a giver, he moved his hands to her fanny, his fingers led by Aneesha's reaction and intensity of moans. He inserted his left index finger deep inside her last orifice and the right hand one inside the one beside it. He could do this despite discomfort because his body was flexible. He was able to run his fingers in and out, pressing the membrane in between with the two index fingers and the tip of her slit. She screamed with excitement until culmination.

This gave him so much relief from the anxiety of not being able to perform that his little one got excited and throbbed as he rubbed it on her fanny vigorously, to come in a big way on her. Both were thoroughly exhausted. He panted like a dog: a sign of loyalty and commitment, she thought.

It was late in the afternoon when they woke up. It took them a while to figure why it was so late.

"You're my hero. How did you give me a big one, yet managed so well for yourself independently?" asked Aneesha.

"In the end analysis, you have sex only with yourself, if you love yourself," replied Shamiq.

"That's so true; you are true only with yourself."

"Yes. I can love myself only after I have been able to satisfy my love."

"You strained yourself so much for me. No one can do what you did. Where did you get so much energy from?"

"I'm just flexible. The more flexible you are, the more positions you can assume to make your circumstances enjoyable."

"What about the discomfort you went through doing that?"

"It gets comfortable after a while and you can enjoy it."

"Wow! To find comfort and enjoyment in discomfort is salvation."

Aneesha's phone rang. It was Harry.

31

Harry Om

Harry called Arjun in Houston. He was relieved to hear that Arjun was busy soliciting business and Natasha sounded positive. He then called Aneesha. She was full of beans. She told him about Shamiq and the things she had discovered about him. Harry passed his phone to Khush when Aneesha enquired about him.

Khush looked pleased as he ended the call. He was all praise for Shamiq and Harry agreed that Shamiq being a masochist, was a real giver. He took pains to give and enjoy at the same time. Harry wondered why masochist was unnecessarily considered derogatory.

Continuing with his train of thought, Harry asked himself why Indians, though talented, weren't equally productive. Perhaps because they were arty, not crafty, he told himself. We are lazy and want to remain in our comfort zone. He broke into a poem.

Discomforts are temporary but comforts are addictive,

Discomforts can be outgrown but comforts are restrictive,

Life is a roller coaster ride that pushes you out of your comfort zone.

You need to stay in control to prevent your brains from being blown.

Accept life the way it is, you must make that effort

To deal with life is to find comfort in discomfort.

Better be uncomfortable in comfort, there's is no gain without pain.

Enjoying discomfort is the salvation that comes with experience for your gain.

Khush was listening keenly. "*Enjoying discomforts is an impossibility. Can you do that?*" he asked.

"*We all can, if we motivate ourselves enough,*" replied Harry.

"*How?*"

"*I have seen you lift heavy weights at the gym. Your expressions reveal the discomfort you go through, lifting them.*"

"*But do I enjoy it?*"

"*But, of course. Otherwise, you'd end up a pot-bellied couch potato. After a heavy workout, when you are completely exhausted, perspiring, and drained, don't you enjoy a hot shower and a hot meal?*"

"*Yes. And the omelettes after we're exhausted from playing tennis.*"

"*As much as I enjoy stretching and deep-tissue massage. Comfort in discomfort!*"

At that moment, Harry's phone rang. It was Anita. Harry told her that he was just thinking about stretching and deep-tissue massage.

"*What are you waiting for?*" asked Anita.

33
Anita and Harry again

Out of sheer habit when in the company of Khush, Harry had put the call on speaker.

"What are we waiting for?" asked Khush.

Harry looked at him and smiled. *"Let's all meet up with Swapna, Shamiq Aneesha and..."*

Khush cut him short. *"Anita won't come because Shamiq will be there, and Sanjib and Anu are busy doing up their house."*

"We'll meet them some other time, but Anita is a nice girl, I'll work on her."

They left CCI immediately. Khush drove Harry to his house as usual and dropped him at the gate, before taking a U-turn to his house in Cuffe Parade, just minutes away. Harry walked to his building. He looked up to see Anita eyeing him admiringly. His blood started to stir as he waved to her.

She opened the door and hugged him, but immediately pushed him away. *"Shit! You're stinking."*

"You called and Khush and I had to skip our shower after an arduous game of tennis. Poor Khush. He has no one to hug him and push him away."

They both started laughing and as Harry headed for the shower, she pulled him back.

"I have the right ingredients to get the stench off," she said, twisting her nostrils with a smile.

Harry was tickled to see her in this mood and when she came forward to give him the special spray, he took it and with the other hand, pulled her stretchy to expose her bottoms.

She immediately pulled them up. *"You're getting young in your old age,"*

"That's hitting under the belt."

"How?"

"It's like reminding a woman of her age; an old man is no different."

"On the contrary, you are the youngest man in the group. No one comes close in reflexes and energy."

Harry made a face and quietly lay down on a thick sheet spread on the carpet, after spraying his body with what smelt of alcohol. He was thoroughly enjoying the fuss, as she bent to wipe his body.

She was so good with stretching every limb in his body and the deep tissue massage that followed that it turned him on. He pulled her down, stripped her and they combined like never before.

She was thoroughly exhausted and lying on her back; she dozed off. Lying next to her in his undies, he planned the rest of the Sunday with a sundowner.

She stirred and opened her eyes. *"Let's have a shower together,"* she said.

Harry moved his loving hands on her bare body. She loved it. Encouraged, he gave her a massage. He felt like a pro as he went about it systematically imitating her. She was in seventh heaven. A deep-tissue massage followed by stretching exhausted Harry.

He realised the effort necessary to give a massage. His massage and stretching were quite intense and discomforting, yet enjoyable and comforting. He cherished the feel-good effect.

"Enough, I'm done!" she said, when she could take it no more. *"The best masseur can't do what you've done for me; you are God-sent for me."*

He planted a kiss on her forehead. When you serve a person, whose life is about serving others, you are serving God.

He lifted her from the floor and made his way to the shower.

34

In the shower

Under the shower, Harry and Anita were examining each other's bodies. Harry went through a feeling of intimacy and closeness that he had not experienced with anyone other than his soulmate Swapna. Probably, these were the rewards for the sacrifices that they had made to keep their attachment away. He dared not turn complacent as taking life for granted could shake up his faith.

"Where are you?" she said, looking down to see why his gaze was stuck on the droplets of water hitting the bathroom floor.

"I was lost in my thoughts, emerging from our closeness, which we cannot take for granted."

"Why not?"

"Because you're too good to be true; this is almost like fiction."

"No, I'm real. Touch me," she said, pulling his hand to her bust. She laughed to see him aroused.

"Let's plan a sundowner today," he suggested.

"Yes. Where?"

"At Gadda Da Vida"

"Oh yes! Beautiful view."

"Let's call everyone there, even Aneesha and Shamiq."

"Why Shamiq?"

"He's Khush's brother-in-law and he's not as you think; he's a good man."

Anita remained silent. She quickly shampooed and conditioned her hair, and soaped her body. Harry tried to keep the conversation going, but Anita didn't reciprocate. Harry cursed himself for ruining the paradise they were in.

Why would he do something this foolish? This was God's way of saving them from another attachment, he realised, a smile appearing on his lips. It was all so true. Enjoy by all means, but do not be attached all over again. Not after learning a lesson the hard way. He could fall in this trap again. God was all about love, not attachment.

He did not even realise that Anita had stepped out of the bathroom, furious that he had not hugged and made up with her. Anita had become dependent on him but he was in no position to reciprocate. At this moment, he was in bliss, connected with the life beyond!

35
Group chat

When Harry finally came out of the shower, he called out to Anita.

Getting no response, he recalled her annoyance. She looked hurt, as she barged out of the bathroom. He picked up his phone to call her and came across several messages on the WhatsApp group chat. Khush, Swapna, and Aneesha already knew about his proposed sundowner at Gadda-Da-Vida that evening. How did this happen? He realised that he had been in the bath far too long, immersed in his thoughts.

The only other person Harry had mentioned this to, was Khush. Anita had told Swapna and Khush had called Shamiq to make a booking. Shamiq was thrilled and he booked an exclusive corner table. Being a much-in-demand DJ, it wasn't difficult for Shamiq to get a reservation at such short notice. Harry always depended on Khush's networking skills for everything and that's how this had started.

Anita was terrified about Harry's plans. She called her well-wisher Swapna, who in turn, tried calling Harry many times but in vain. She got busy on the group chat. Khush and Aneesha joined in. They awaited Harry's response. He was the last person to respond on the chat.

Harry: Great job Khush! And Swapna, looks like I've had a tiff with Anita. Please bail me out and make sure she comes.

Khush: It was a great thought. Let's enjoy. Please get Anita.

Aneesha: Anita must come! Shamiq is not going to trouble her; he's my younger bro.

Swapna: Okay, honey, leave her to me.

Harry: Thanks, guys. Please pick me up at four pm. Khush, God bless.

36
In-a-Gadda-Da-Vida

The place was simply beautiful and to everyone's surprise, not only did Anita, but Anu and Sanjib turned up too at Gadda-da-Vida, Juhu. The two, who were busy doing up their Worli house, needed a break. Anita came with Swapna and Khush drove Harry, Aneesha, and Shamiq to the venue.

Shamiq – a sound engineer - was the host of this grand get-together. He was a millionaire with his twenty per cent shareholding in his late father's closely-held company. With fifty per cent holding, his sister was the CMD, and her husband Khush held the rest. In the past decade with his ingenuity alone, the company's worth had risen fifteen times over.

Khush had taken charge of his late friend Shom Bhatia's company and was grooming Shom's son to take over from him. Khush's son was 35 years old and the CEO of his mother's company.

It was an hour to sunset and drinks were being served. Shamiq was sitting with Aneesha on one side of a big square table, and Anu was sandwiched between Sanjib and Anita at the opposite end. Harry was with Swapna and Khush opted for sitting with his back to the sea, so that Harry and Swapna could sit together facing it.

"Thank you Khush for being so considerate," said Harry.

"I'd like to know more about your past as it is never enough. More so, your Calcutta stories," replied Khush.

"We all want to know that bit," added Swapna.

All of them were curious, especially the Calcuttans, Anu and Sanjib. Except Anita, who appeared to be deep in thought. She excused herself and walked out to the beach adjoining the restaurant. She's probably not comfortable with Shamiq being the host, thought Harry. Swapna sensed this too. Anita walking on the beach reminded them of Raima.

Khush was the only one in the group with his back to the sea. But now Anita did likewise. Was it because she wanted to escape Shamiq's glare, wondered Harry. Khush felt a gentle touch on his shoulders and turned back to see Anita smiling as she sat beside him.

Anita was no stranger to Khush. He was her very first encounter at the massage parlour before he introduced her to Raima's heartbroken Shom. She looked at Khush who had cared so much for his friend Shom that he had sacrificed his relationship with her for Shom's sake. In Natasha's absence, she needed a companion like Khush. More so because Harry was dividing his attention between Swapna and her. Anita was about to say something when Shamiq interrupted her thoughts.

37

2020

As Anita was about to say something Shamiq interrupted blurting, *"There's nothing new about your changing positions and partners. I'm not the only one you've betrayed."*

Everyone was startled. Anita turned red and she exploded, *"That was completely unwarranted, Shamiq."*

Shamiq immediately corrected himself. He realised that he'd have to bear the brunt of his foolhardy behaviour.

"He is such a creep," said Anita to Swapna. *"I was reluctant to come here in the first place."*

"Yes. I am repenting for having coaxed you to come here," replied Swapna.

Aneesha butted in, *"He's the best I have ever known. Women love the company of such people. Don't call him a creep."*

Harry added, *"Yes, women are attracted to gays because they are comfortable with them. Moreover, they jell better as they are not of the opposite sex."*

"However, there are men who understand women very well," replied Swapna.

"They are the special ones from the old school who even write romance. Most men cannot distinguish between love and the other four-letter word," said Aneesha.

"Let's stop discussing all this on the last day of the decade," concluded Harry.

Khush agreed. *"Oh yeah! Where do we go after the sun goes down?"*

"I have a few options but the traffic is going to be a big turnoff. It would be better to get back early," replied Harry.

Swapna said, *"What's the point in stepping out on such days? I would like to stay the night with Harry."*

"I love that," said Harry. *"Let's finish dinner here and meet up to ring in 2020. For a change let's be amongst people on the other side of the shore."*

"With people on the ships you see from your window. The lights from ships reflecting in the sea look beautiful," responded Khush.

Shamiq was repenting for being rudely blunt. Thrilled to spot him, a group of youngsters came up to him. He led them to the beach and Aneesha followed. There was a sigh of relief on Anita's face. Harry and Khush got into a conversation. There was a clear divide within the group with regard to Shamiq.

A person who speaks his mind will evoke extreme reactions, thought Harry. *"In today's world there's no time for small talk. Let's fight for progress instead of finding fault with one another,"* he said.

"It is sunset time," called out Shamiq, signalling them to move forward, as the orange ball, no longer fiery, dipped into the sea. It looked like a giant orange submerging submarine, now just a hemi-head, and then just the top, and in a split second, nothing. The 'submarine' was underwater, but its glow was visible in the sky, bright orange with streaks of red and purple. Sanjib and Anu lead the brigade as they walked along the shore with Harry, Swapna, Khush, and Anita.

Shamiq and Aneesha joined the party back in the restaurant for an early dinner before all of them headed to Harry's house in Colaba. Anita stayed with Harry, but that night being the New Decade Night, Swapna had decided to be with Harry. It would take her a couple of hours to return to her apartment at Napean Sea Road through the traffic.

Anita felt left out, she'd never seen this side of Harry. He seemed hooked on to Swapna, she thought. Where do I go? Not Khush.

That's when Swapna drew her attention by taking her hand in hers and said, *"May I share your room like I did with Raima?"*

38
Dance by the bay

Harry was sitting in the front seat next to the chauffeur, with Anita and Swapna at the rear. With two women on his back at the same time, he was in a dilemma. A part of him was overjoyed with Swapna's decision. Another part was heartbroken. Being with his soulmate at the end of the year was special, but they had company.

As he turned back, he saw Swapna whisper something in Anita's ear. He was glad that the two of them got along well. Khush was following them with Shamiq and Aneesha. Anu and Sanjib had to rush back home to prepare for their house-warming brunch the following day, the first day of the decade. Invitations had been extended to the group that evening.

The bay windows in Harry's apartment offered a 220 degrees view of the harbour. Conscious of his foolishness earlier in the evening, Shamiq was subdued. Anita stopped thinking about him, concentrating on her own issues with Harry. Khush, Swapna, and Anita got cracking with dessert cocktails.

The music was soothing. Swapna pulled Harry up for a dance to her favourite song by Louis Armstrong, *What a Wonderful World*. They were lost to the world.

Khush and Anita felt awkward about getting intimate with each other, as both had been close to their departed friend Shom. Shamiq and Aneesha felt a bit out of place. Particularly because Shamiq was trying to be extra civil with Anita. Anita, on the other hand, was noticing him for the first time. She discovered that he had changed from the time they had their first encounter a decade ago, the memory of which was loathsome. She asked how he was able to attract so many women to himself. Clearly embarrassed, he thought it was because he was a giver, a masochist, unlike a macho male who is a sadist.

Anita said that she would have to figure that out. She kept swaying her body to the beats, prompting Shamiq to react. Soon, they were the second couple on the floor; Khush and Aneesha followed suit.

At the stroke of midnight, the pyrotechnics illuminated the sky. Soulmates Harry and Swapna were lip-locked and lost to the world. Only those who are lost to the world find themselves. Shamiq whispered New Year greetings in Anita's ears, their arms around each other, and their spirits buoyant.

39

A change of heart

Shamiq whispered New Year greetings in Anita's ears, their arms around each other, and their spirits buoyant. Anita felt the sensation and responded likewise.

Their lips were a whispering distance from each other's ear lobes. Anita turned her face and their lips made contact. Shamiq took in her lips and tongue.

The lights came on and Swapna greeted everyone. Anita excused herself and to everyone's surprise, led Shamiq to her bedroom. Harry smiled, as if he had expected this radical change of heart.

Khush was relieved to have Aneesha back. They merrily held each other's hand as they set off for Khush's house. Harry was relieved to be with the love of his life.

What about Anita without Harry and Shamiq without Aneesha? Anita and Shamiq's first encounter years ago had left a scar that was yet to heal. It was Anita's first exposure to sex in her early teens and Shamiq's first encounter with a woman.

"Why this change of heart? You called me a creep," enquired Shamiq.

"You were a creep a decade ago and that's how I know you," replied Anita.

"And so?"

"You've changed a lot."

"And so?"

Their expressions said it all. Before Shamiq could reply, Anita pulled him up close. He removed her top and went for her right lobe. Taking it fully in his mouth while pressing and massaging the left one. He moved the tip of his tongue to needle her nipple. This was the ultimate turn on for Anita, who moaned with ecstasy.

He moved on to the other one before going down to eat out the pussy. Their pleasure peaked. He pierced his hard-on and she screamed with pleasure. Shamiq rose to his greatness, realising that he could perform only if he gave it all. He was a giver in the truest sense of the word.

40

01.01.2020

The first day of the new decade was a holiday, Harry woke up rather grudgingly although it was past 11:30, and there was Swapna with a glass of fresh orange juice in her hand.

"Honey, have a heart we slept only after sunrise," he pleaded.

"Aren't we going for brunch to Anu's house?" replied Swapna.

"A brunch party on New Year's Day? This is ridiculous! We've slept for only four hours."

"Don't behave like a child, Harry! We accepted their invite. It's their home show, the opening ceremony on the first day of the year. Let's think of a gift for them."

"Why don't we all pool in for the gift?"

"Great idea. Let's give them something for the new house. I'll figure that out when I talk to Anu."

"Very nice! Hey, this drink is great, what is it, love?"

"It's an immediate cure for people who have over-indulged and are woken up. I'm sorry, had no choice."

"Orange juice with garlic and something else?"

"Yes, garlic juice plus a large peg of lime juice, well-shaken."

Swapna reached out for the phone to call Anu. There were messages on the group chat requesting that the brunch be changed to dinner. This brought a smile on Swapna's face. *'Thanks, Harry and I were about to suggest it,'* she posted. A little later Khush and Aneesha too opted for dinner.

Swapna called Anu. Thanks to Raima, they shared a close bond. Swapna had once dropped by at Anu's new apartment on her way to Bandra via the sea link. A casual conversation had led to Swapna providing some valuable inputs regarding the house décor, and a sense of bonding between them.

Shamiq and Anita woke up at 1.45 pm and were relieved to hear about the change of plan. Swapna and Anita got busy finding a matching couch with side tables for Anu's hall and located one in Lower Parel, a stone's throw from Worli. They all looked at a picture on the phone and approved of the gift.

"What are the damages and what's my share?" enquired Shamiq.

"Rs 48000 plus GST. Only the men and I as the initiator contribute. That's Rs 12000 each, plus GST," replied Swapna.

Everyone nodded in approval. Swapna wrote out a cheque and sent it to the furniture store.

After the heavy meal, they all felt a snooze was a must to gear up for yet another late night. Swapna went home to change, as did Shamiq, but he lived next door. It was planned that Harry would fetch Swapna from her Napean Sea Road apartment and the two of them would proceed to Worli.

Shamiq took Anita to a couple massage at Four Seasons. This was a treat for Anita who worked as a masseuse and was now being served by one.

After the massage, the two massage tables were joined to each other like a double bed. They lay on their backs, their nude bodies covered by a thin sheet of linen.

The masseuse placed Anita's right hand on Shamiq's left and departed after wishing the couple some romantic moments. The lights had been dimmed and Bob Dylan's *'Lay, Lady, Lay'* played in the background.

41

Worli-Bandra Sea Link

The couple massage was sensual. It acted as a catalyst for lovemaking. Shamiq discovered his physical abilities to be a giver in the real sense of the word. He performed his penance by satisfying the person he had failed, years earlier. He went all out. Although a prolonged one-sided excruciation, he being a masochist, enjoyed the process. Going down on a woman, especially someone as young and robust as Anita, lead to an explosive reaction between her fluid and his saliva.

The ultimate pleasure of culmination on her face confirmed that he was indeed serving his goddess. The very thought gave him a hard-on. He immersed into her, resulting in a volcanic peak for both, one after the other. He felt as though his goddess was helping him attain salvation. Anita too was utterly exhausted. She hugged him tightly and took a catnap.

By the time they were through with the Jacuzzi steam and shower, it was quite late, and they needed a change of clothes for Anu and Sanjib's party. They rushed to the Palladium mall where Anita picked up a high-split surplice velvet cami dress, at the AND store, and Shamiq purchased a trendy shirt and a pair of trousers with a waistcoat to go with it.

When they reached Anu's place, everyone else was already there and the congratulatory buzz for the housewarming was over. Anu and Sanjib thanked the guests for the three-seater couch. The way it had been arranged in the room with a beautiful view of the Worli-Bandra Sea Link as the backdrop, was aesthetically pleasing.

The guests went gaga over Anita's elegant gown. When they all settled down, there were no takers for the alcoholic drinks as they had all had more than their fill the previous evening. Everything was going smoothly, thought Anu, but Sanjib felt something was amiss. He needed a mood-enhancer.

As if reading his thoughts, Harry said, *"To relieve our minds of the pressures of life or to seek altered consciousness, we use external influences such as a counsellor or an intoxicant."*

"Right! A stimulant. Should we smoke up?" asked Sanjib.

He pulled out a few joints and Khush joined in. *"We had too many downers yesterday, today we go for the uppers,"* he said.

"Cannabis is nature's mildest herb, a mind changer. How to make it work for us without getting addicted to it is up to us. Ironic that addictions such as alcohol and tobacco that have nothing beneficial are legal to sell and consume," said Harry.

"What about tea and coffee?" asked Swapna.

"Mild stimulants and therefore, addictive," replied Harry.

"What about Coke?" asked Anita.

"That's a difficult one to answer, as in the year 1929 Coca-Cola drink became cocaine-free. But I don't know what they've done to make Coke addictive," answered Harry.

Much to Anu's surprise, Sanjib fished out some joints he had rolled himself. Sanjib said that it was legal in the place where he'd come from, and his boss had gotten him into the habit to create abstracts used for conducting experiments to innovate products. Anu herself did not go beyond the occasional glass of wine.

Shamiq had quietly slipped out to the balcony to admire the sea link. He had graduated to snorting coke. Aneesha noticed it as her eyes followed him all evening. Anita rose suddenly and made her way to the balcony, with everyone's eyes following her.

42

Bindaas!

With Aneesha and Anita cornering Shamiq, there was something to worry about here, thought Harry, as he watched the proceedings unfold.

Aneesha was close to Shamiq. She saw Anita approaching them, giving her a dirty look. Anita could never fathom Aneesha. Her emotions were of a she-male, and the male side of her surfaced to put Anita in her place. She pounced on Shamiq.

"Give me some of that, I need it," demanded Anita.

"Shamiq, not in this house and certainly not with a novice like Anita. She's capable of flying off the balcony," intervened Harry.

"Sure, Harry. I don't have anything left," said Shamiq, winking as he crossed Harry.

Sanjib came forward to pass a joint to Harry and said, *"I got into this stuff from my school days in Calcutta."*

"Which school did you go to?" asked Harry.

"South Point, the best school in my time."

"I was there for six years, 20 years before you."

"How was the school in those days?"

"It was comparatively new and the only co-ed school, and this stuff," said Harry, pointing to the joint before passing it to Swapna. *"This was not around till I did some research and found out about pot or cannabis that American kids were so crazy about. I read about it in western books."*

Anu announced dinner and everyone made a beeline for the table. *"We're not planning any kids at our age. So we intend to extend the hall by demolishing the partition wall when we do up the house next."*

The dining table was placed at right angles to the balcony with a view of the sea link. Harry, Swapna, and Anita sat on one side of the table, with Swapna in between. But Anita detested this as Shamiq was away from her, sitting beside Aneesha, who was giving her a lot of grief by defying her attitude.

"Harry, what did you find in the library?" enquired Khush.

"About the herb called bhaang in Hindi. I made twenty joints and my friend and I smoked up everything without any effect; no high, just huff and puff. We went complaining to the vendor next to the temple, where we came across a sadhu. He made me smoke his chillum. I pulled on it hard and coughed. The vendor realised what we wanted, and he gave us ganja."

"That's great," exclaimed Sanjib.

"Have you heard the word 'bindaas'?" asked Khush.

"Yes, on TV, but I don't know what it means."

"Harry knows where and how it originated. Tell us, Harry."

Anita butted in, to break free of Aneesha's spell. *"A woman who doesn't care what people think about her skimpy attire is called bindaas."*

"My family shifted to Bombay in the early 1960s, when I was in my mid-teens. At that time there used to be a place called Napoli's, on the sea face," said Harry.

"You mean where Pizza Hut is today?" asked Khush.

"No! There was nothing there. Talk-of-the-Town came up in the late 1960s. Napoli's was on the opposite side of the road, on the seafront."

"Which is now a promenade?" asked Anita.

"There was no footpath or road at that time; it was more of a dead end."

"What about Gaylord?" asked Swapna.

"Gaylord, Berry's and Bombelli's were all there with live bands, but Napoli's was a tiny place with a jukebox and a collection of my favourites. I would insert a 25 paise coin and get to listen to three songs. 'Take Five' and 'These Boots are Made for Walking' were my regular choices. This was much before I set my eyes on you, Swapna."

"So what happened, who did you meet there?" enquired Sanjib.

"Dr Kanitkar. He loved music and he was a poet, and 15 years older. We became buddies. We would smoke up while sipping coffee and listening to the songs. Our favourite was 'I Wanna Hold Your Hand'

by the Beatles. The entire restaurant would go thumping and we never had to pay for it, someone or the other always did."

"Why aren't you people eating?" interjected Anu.

"Of course, we're all enjoying your food," replied Khush.

"Ami to dal bhaat aar chingree mach ta khabo. Khubi bhalo," said Harry.

They all had a hearty laugh.

"Tell us about bindaas," said Khush.

"Dr Alagamuthu Kanitkar; we called him Doc because his first name was difficult to pronounce. More than a doctor, he was a patient, a cancer patient from childhood who refused to undergo chemotherapy. He just wanted to live his life and after a few months, he started bringing his daughter Sonal along. Or perhaps, Sonal used to bring him to keep him amused. In any case, the ambience was for college kids and Sonal would bunk her first year Commerce classes at Sydenham College, which was a stone's throw away."

"Oh my God! Poor Doc," said Swapna.

"Doc would often use the word bindaas when he was high. His lovely eyes would twinkle as he smiled. We all got into the habit of using that word in our conversations. One day Doc and Sonal stopped coming to Napoli's. We were disheartened. None of us knew where they stayed. Sonal wasn't attending her classes either. My visits to Napoli's petered off. A year later, I met Sonal at a friend's party. She told me that her dad had died in her arms. It was a peaceful death. That's when I came to know more about the man and how pure he

was. Sonal told me that the Marathi word 'bindhast' meant 'fearless' or 'carefree'."

"What about his wife?" asked Swapna.

"We did not go into those details. He outlived her by ten years. Going by Sonal's looks, her mother must have been beautiful. 'Bindaas', as it stands today, has no definite meaning; it is freedom from the controlled mind."

"So when you smoke up, are you bindaas?" asked Sanjib.

"Not necessarily, you can also get paranoid. It is a state of mind that becomes more flexible, and therefore gives you the liberty to alter between the free mind and the controlled one. You need a mastermind to get the best of both. Doc had that mastermind as he lived on the edge and balanced the two. He achieved the golden mean between the free mind and the controlled one. Sonal told me that his last smile said it all, as he uttered bindaas for the last time."

43

Lost to the world

Anu and Sanjib's party continued past midnight before they all decided to call it a night. Harry accompanied Swapna to her apartment, at Napean Sea Road. With Natasha away, as she was studying in Houston, the flat was vacant. Khush took Aneesha home and Shamiq went along with Anita.

Once in the car, Swapna came up with an unexpected query. *"Where's Sonal now?"*

"I have no idea," replied Harry. *"I last met her more than fifty years ago. We've had no contact."*

"Were the two of you in a relationship?"

"We loved each other's company, and we both got serious about our studies. I was studying engineering in Baroda and gradually we lost touch. There were no mobile phones at that time."

"Did she get married?"

"I hope so, though she was not the marrying kind. Her dad had made enough money and left enough property for her. He lived in the hope that she would get married, but alas, he did not live that long. She's an independent sort and very stable. She would correct me in many ways when we lived together for a year and a half before she went

to her aunt in New Jersey for her graduation. At Sydenham College, she would attend the lectures she liked, but did not complete her B.Com. Course. I could see that she was working hard for something she did not tell me about. She used to be highly critical of doctors and medical researchers for not finding a cure for cancer. She would echo her dad's views that a doctor's job is to teach, not treat. Suppressing the disease is all we know. It amounts to a moneymaking racket for them, drug manufacturers, and researchers. Drugs with multiple side effects suppress the disease but it revives with a vengeance."

"She seemed to have made an impression on you."

"Yes. She was intelligent, interesting, and loving."

"How many affairs have you had?"

"Not many, after we had to breakup after a decade."

"That was tragic but we outgrew our attachment, and what remains is pure love. I love you because you love the world."

"Muhabbat sirf ek se kyun, Khuda to hum sab mein hai. Muhabbat Khuda hai, ye elaan har mazhab mein hai."

"Wah! You're such a pet." Swapna hugged Harry and he responded by kissing her.

They spent the night together in bliss, entangled under a quilt. After a late breakfast the next morning, both set off for work.

Tragedy struck the following morning. Harry was in the shower, grooving to the music playing at full blast when he slipped on the soap, hit his head on the shower mixer tap, and fell unconscious on the floor.

A little later Anita and Shamiq came to the house to collect Anita's personal effects. They came unannounced as Harry wouldn't answer the doorbell nor answer the phone. Anita went about packing her clothes in her bags. Shamiq noticed water gushing out from under the bathroom door. They banged on the door but to no avail. Anita opened it with the door key and screamed her head off at the sight inside.

Shamiq came to the rescue. He turned off the tap and called Khush. An ambulance was called for. Khush and Swapna arrived and between all of them, they carried Harry to his bedroom. Khush pumped him back to life. The ambulance arrived soon. Swapna grabbed on to Harry, whispering in his ears, as tears trickled down her cheeks. There was no reaction. All seemed to be over. Harry was dead to the world.

44

Identity crisis

The rain was persistent. He could hear it drumming on the cement sheet roof of the workshop shed. Swallowing his saliva to moisten his parched throat, he wondered if they'd bring him some food and water, and wondered again if they'd come at all. Placing an empty bucket on his head, he stepped out in the rain. The bucket shielded him from the rain and the water filling in it would quench his thirst. With the wind falling silent, the droplets fell straight into the bucket. His head hurt with the increasing weight of the water. Feeling a bruise where it hurt, he rushed back into the shelter of the roof shed and placing the bucket on the floor, started licking the water like a dog.

No sooner, he quenched his thirst than he heard approaching footsteps and voices. He tried to get up but failed. As a figure drew close, he struck the person on the head with the bucket. He heard more voices that faded away as drowsiness sets in. He wondered whether he was dying.

As he opened his eyes, everything around was white and clean. The air felt pure and tinged with a sweet fragrance. A gentle feminine face appeared in his field of vision. Caring hands caressed his cheeks. As the hands lingered a bit, he extended his hands to hold on to them. Surprisingly, there was no resistance, encouraging his advance. Grabbing the hands, he drew the woman up close, feeling her warm breath on his face. Releasing herself from his grip, she pushed a thermometer into his mouth.

He heard someone behind the woman ask, *"How's Harry doing?"*

Who was Harry, he wondered. Was it him? He was unable to remember his name, or for that matter, anything about himself.

"It's a case of psychological trauma. So far, he hasn't spoken a word," said another voice.

The thermometer was pulled out of his mouth and he saw the group of people in white coats behind the woman, talking among themselves.

One of them came up and examined the back of his head. He felt a dull pain when a finger was placed at a particular point.

"Harry, how do you feel? Do you want to get up?" asked the person.

He found his voice but could not recall anything. Why was he there? Why did they not bring him food and water? Seeing him agitated, the doctor told a nurse to calm him down.

The gentle face reappeared in his line of vision. He looked around. The room was big and luxurious. The staff apart, he seemed to be the only person there. He liked the thought of the nurse being in attendance. Was she going to be with him all the time; he certainly didn't want to be alone!

He sat up on the bed to get the attention he sought. The woman sat beside him, concerned, yet smiling. There is passion and sincerity in her ways. He wondered why he couldn't recall his identity. Was it because identity was the root cause of all evil? Now that he didn't have one, was he not free of ego? Who was footing his bill? How long would these people look after him? What did he do for a living? These questions pounded his mind.

The woman held his hands and lovingly said, *"Don't worry so much, what's bothering you?"*

"I don't know who I am." he replied.

"Don't worry. Just enjoy this time and experience of having no responsibilities, no pressure. Identify with your heart and its purity."

"Does anyone want to live without responsibility?"

"Forget responsibilities and obligation, you're better off living for your passions."

"That makes sense. I wish I knew you from before."

"You know me now."

"Not when I don't even know myself."

"You only don't have an identity, try to know yourself, the inner self."

"That's easy to say. What happens when life catches up on me? Who's paying for my treatment and what happened to me?"

"Too many questions, we'll go one by one."

"Are you a psychiatrist? Or a nurse?"

"Both! I'm an intern specialising in psychiatry, and here to nurse you."

"Oh no! Does it mean I am mentally unstable?"

"You are suffering from amnesia. But don't worry, it's a mild head trauma, which requires no medical treatment."

"When will I recover? You're not telling me anything. I have asked you many questions."

"Please calm down, I'll tell you all that I know."

"Your name is Harry and I know your metabolic age because we generally check all that, it's 51."

"That old? Tell me more about Harry."

"I don't know who Harry is, except that he's rich or well-connected enough to be in this room of Jaslok Hospital."

"When will I get my memory back?"

"My experience and qualifications tell me that your brain is quite sharp and alert, your metabolic age is in your favour. The less anxious you are, the faster you will recover."

"Thanks. When will I meet the people, who brought me here?"

"My seniors will decide. My job is to write a daily report of your recovery. Two iPhones were found in your jacket pockets, one will recognise your fingerprint, and the other, your face. You'll be able to know everything about yourself. It may even bring back your memory."

"Please give me my phones. But what is an iPhone?"

"Only when you're ready for it will my seniors give these to you. We'll make better progress if you try to answer my questions."

He was about to speak, but she stopped him by placing her finger on his lips.

"No more questions. Now put your anxiety to rest and calm down. It's time for lunch," she said, pressing a button.

He raised a finger. She raised her eyebrows and asked, *"What now?"*

"Just one last question. I don't even know your name. It's impolite to ask a woman her age, but a pretty woman must have a name."

She smiled and said, *"I'm Dr Sheila Dikshit and my metabolic age is 20."*

Before he could react, the door opened and the food trolley was wheeled in. His mouth began to water.

45
My Swapna

Harry waited in a café. The mood was gloomy. He was meeting Swapna for the last time. Ten years of their relationship was ending. He wasn't sure how Swapna was going to react, or for that matter, whether she would turn up at all. When she arrived, he tried to read her face, but it was blank, with traces of hurt. They sat in complete silence until Harry called the waiter for their usual stuff and mocha coffee. Still silent, she looked everywhere but at him. Done with the coffee, one of them was yet to make the first move. The café was almost empty. His decision was heart-breaking. He wanted the attachment to die and love to remain unhindered.

He felt their relationship was baseless; he was long married and she was only twenty years old. Her father - a millionaire - wanted her to marry a tycoon's son. And he was a mere struggler. He had to rush to his workshop, which was just a roof shed with some in-house machinery. He hoped they would be done with this gracefully.

Aware of his stealing glances, she looked at him and asked, *"What's on your mind?"*

Harry's face brightened up. *"The best we can do is not be dependent on each other; dependence degrades our love to the level of attachment. Let's aim to become independent, so that we are proud of each other. This way we will be able to remember our years of association as a means of growth that resulted in respect and acceptance. True love is not confined to a single relationship. It gives us the liberty to change from one to the other, to suit the circumstances. We should not enslave ourselves to our needs. Let's lead a guilt-free life and protect your dad from knowing about us, lest he collapses and dies of heart failure. We will not weaken; instead rise in love to derive energy. We will demonstrate our strengths to the world to acquire the freedom we want."*

She looked at him but chose not to reply. Harry was glad she didn't respond angrily. He tried to make eye contact, but she kept staring at the ceiling. Eventually, she looked at him in the eye and said, *"We should be going now."*

Harry felt reassured, but didn't know what was going to happen next. Women had a mind of their own, he believed. So far, so good! Then she turned to face him, both looked at each other and an unintended smile appeared on her lips. This was a spiritual encounter, thought Harry, an endorsement that gave them the confidence they needed. They hugged like never before, and parted. Harry thanked God. He realised that breakups happen in relationships, never in love. There were no breakups in love!

46

My Harry

Swapna was still in a state of shock. A week had gone by; the doctors had no answer and no one was allowed to visit. She was angry with herself for letting Harry go back alone. She realised that it was not possible for her to survive without him. Did that mean attachment couldn't be conquered? Love and attachment couldn't be separated and detached attachment was only in theory, not in practise? They had struggled for years for the sake of their love and the end-result had been so jarring.

Her thoughts went back to the day they had broken up. He had broken up for her sake and she had grudged it. She could have put her foot down and not allowed the breakup to happen. They would have defied the world and eloped. She cursed herself for harbouring such thoughts. She felt dizzy as she stood up to answer Natasha calling from Houston. Still not in the right frame of mind, she heard Natasha rattling away without grasping a word.

When Anu and Sanjib came over, she was incoherent. Khush was struggling to get the doctors to allow a visit, but the request was turned down. He was told that there was very little hope. Not wanting to cause further grief to Swapna, he kept the news to himself. Anita cursed herself for not being with Harry on the day of his fall. Unlike others, Aneesha was hopeful. She told Khush not to lose heart; nothing could happen to a man like Harry.

Then one day as Swapna woke up feeling weak from lack of sleep, she saw Harry, as if speaking to her. It was a daydream that left a deep imprint. She felt an uncontrollable urge to be with him. Every bit of her longed for him. He was hers forever. She was going to be his, look after him, and be with him all the time. With that resolve, her spirits soared. She got up, energy returning to her being.

47

A new beginning

He opened his eyes to find Sheila in a conference with the men in white. After they left, Sheila came to him with a reassuring smile.

"My God, you're so beautiful, you're my Swapna," he said.

"Who's she?" asked Sheila.

"Swapna means dream; you're my swapna come true. My dream come true."

"Tell me everything; I'm your doctor cum nurse. That allows me some liberty," she said, giving him a peck on his lips.

Harry told her everything about Swapna.

"What else do you remember?"

"My work. I remember my workshop on Thane–Belapur Road."

"How long ago was that?"

"I don't know."

"Can you recall any national event?"

"Demonetisation?" said Harry after some thought.

"You mean the one in 1978?"

"Okay. I remember now. Swapna and I met just before Woodstock 1969 and we parted ten years later."

"That was a long time ago. You don't look that old."

"How old am I today?"

She handed him over two phones.

"What are these?"

"Mobile phones."

"Mobile phones?"

"Yes, they are fully charged."

"What am I supposed to do?"

"This is your identity."

Harry fiddled with one of them before Sheila switched one on and held it in front of his face. The display lit up with an image of him.

"This is me!"

"Yes. Your face is your password, your identity. Your other phone accepts your thumbprint as a password. We'll try that later."

"What do you call these mobile phones?"

"Because you can talk to or text anyone in the world from just about anywhere. It is connected to the internet."

"What is the internet?"

"An international network of all the mobile phones and computers in the world connected through a global computer network providing a variety of information and communication facilities, consisting of interconnected networks using standardised communication protocols."

"Oh my God, the world has advanced so much in my absence. How will I catch up?"

"Not so difficult. Our entire knowledge is available on Google and Wikipedia."

"What are you talking about? It's all Greek to me."

"Don't be anxious. You will recover your memory. There's been a lot of progress in just a few days."

"Please help me get back my Swapna. I want her now." Harry broke down in Sheila's arms.

As the days progressed, Harry and Sheila made headway with their individual missions. He found new ways to flirt with Sheila, a woman half his age. It was challenging and thrilling, and kept his anxiety at bay. She didn't seem to mind it and even went all the way with him.

"I'm just a dirty old man," he blustered out one day.

"Why do you say that?"

"Because..."

"There is no 'because' here! It's nothing to do with us. This is God's desire, the God in you and in me, our purity, our bliss, and our souls."

"You look beautiful."

"I love it when you speak your heart out," she said, blushing.

"You remind me of my soulmate Swapna. We have separated. I run a tiny workshop. I'm passionate about my work and her. These are the two passions of my life. I don't know why I'm here."

"Now's is the time to find out."

"You are so right when you say I should make the best use of this carefree time forced on me. I must look forward and keep my anxiety away."

She nodded lovingly and caressed his cheeks.

A few days later, Harry was allowed to visit his factory. They told him that he headed an engineering company with three factories located on highways. He also had a huge following on social media. This information was gathered from his mobile phones. It was difficult for him to fathom the advances technology had made. With this gadget in his palm, it felt like having the world in his pocket.

One of the doctors accompanied him. They drove directly to the shop floor where they were given safety helmets and eye protectives to wear. The sight of a fancy machine shop, a huge workshop of four long bays, and a team of busy workmen made him envious of the person who owned the place. As he moved closer, he realised that the workmen were at attention, as if he was the owner. Approaching the end of one of the bays, he lost his calm on noticing the operator of a machine use it incorrectly.

Old memories came rushing back to him. He knew this machine! It was a big size VLT that he had refurbished from scrap. Inspecting the gearbox, he recalled picking it up from Daru Khana. It had once been part of a trailer. He had retrofitted it on this machine to give it a sturdy drive. This recollection was a miracle indeed. Gradually, one memory after another came rushing back. The entire place belonged to him, just as he belonged to this place.

The doctor helped him to get into the car and they drove off. Harry's mind was racing as he started to remember everything. He finally knew who he was. He recalled slipping on the soapy water in the shower and hurting himself on the head as he fell to the floor and passed out.

The doctor was pleased with his recovery. The rainwater he thought he had licked like a dog had in fact been water in the shower. He had lain on the bathroom floor of his Colaba apartment for eight hours before they had found him. The doctor also told him that his memories of Swapna, his first workshop and his first pet dog Boozo had kept him alive.

Harry picked up his phone and called Swapna. She was thrilled to hear his voice and told him that Arjun, Khush, and she were in the car following his. They stopped and got together.

"This is a miracle after a nightmarish fortnight," she said.

Dr Sheila had made this recovery possible. Harry felt indebted to her and made up his mind to do something for her in return. She had given him back his old life, but with a new beginning. He hugged Swapna tightly, never wanting to leave her ever again.

9 789355 591364